Skating Stories

Skating Stories

By E. F. Benson

Edited by B. A. Thurber

____

Skating History Press

Main text originally published between 1888 and 1926.
Introduction and notes © 2020 B. A. Thurber.
All rights reserved.

Cover image: "Beautiful Red Sky Matterhorn in Switzerland" by Klausdie. Courtesy of Good Free Photos.
Author photo: Benson at 27 from *Our Family Affairs, 1867–1896* (New York: George H. Doran, c. 1921). Courtesy of Wikimedia Commons.

ISBN: 978-1-948100-07-6
LCCN: 2019920929

Skating History Press
Evanston, IL
http://www.skatinghistorypress.com/

Contents

List of Figures

Introduction

An Inveterate Skater

Edward Frederic Benson (July 24, 1867–February 29, 1940) is well-known for his novels and short stories. He's the author of the Mapp and Lucia series and numerous supernatural tales, which he called "spook stories." He was also an enthusiastic figure skater. His book on skating, *English Figure Skating: A Guide to the Theory and Practice of Skating in the English Style* (London: G. Bell and Sons, 1908), ranked, along with Henry C. Lowther's three-volume collection,[1] as the best of many books on English skating in the first decade of the twentieth century. In it, he "leads the learner from the premier pas to the final coup de théâtre, like a Dodo turned governess."[2]

There is no need for more than a brief sketch of Benson's life here due to the preponderance of full biographies.[3] Fred, as he was commonly known, was the fifth of six children (four boys and two girls) born to Edward

---

1. Henry C. Lowther, *English Skating: Edges and Striking, Principle of Skating Turns, Combined Figure Skating*, ed. B. A. Thurber (Evanston, IL: Skating History Press, 2019). First published in 1900 and 1902.

2. A. E. Crawley, "English Figure-Skating," *The Saturday Review of Politics, Literature, Science and Art* 116 (February 1913): 235; Dodo is the heroine of one his popular series.

3. See, for example, Brian Masters, *The Life of E. F. Benson* (London: Chatto and Windus, 1991) and, for information on his entire family, Simon Goldhill, *A Very Queer Family Indeed: Sex, Religion, and the Bensons in Victorian Britain* (Chicago: University of Chicago Press, 2016).

White Benson, who eventually became Archbishop of Canterbury, and Minnie Sidgwick. He began writing while a student at Marlborough College and continued at Cambridge University. He wrote both fiction and non-fiction, including autobiographical works, for the rest of his life. *Sketches from Marlborough* (Marlborough: Chas. Perkins, 1888), the source of the first story in this volume, is based on his time at Marlborough College, and *The Babe, B.A.: Being the Uneventful History of a Young Gentleman at Cambridge University* (New York: G. P. Putnam's Sons, 1896) takes place in Cambridge.

Like writing, skating was a lifelong passion of Benson's. In *Our Family Affairs*, he describes his early experience with this winter delight:

> ...after lunch we skated on dreadful skates called "Acmes" or "Caledonians," which clipped themselves on to the heels and soles of the boot, and came off and slithered across the ice at the moment when you proposed to execute a turn. [Younger brother] Hugh despised my figure-skating (and I'm sure I don't wonder) and christened himself a speed skater. The pond was of no great extent and fringed on one side by tall rhododendron thickets, into which he crashed when unable to negotiate a corner.[4]

As Benson grew up, he improved substantially. He passed the first-class test—the highest level of achieve-

---

4. Benson, *Our Family Affairs, 1867–1896*, 175–176.

ment—in the English style in Davos, Switzerland, in 1893 and joined the National Skating Association in 1900.[5] Then, he became a judge and was added to both the list of first-class judges and the emergency judges' list. Judges on the latter list are able to nominate qualified people to judge when needed.

Like many wealthy English citizens, Benson enjoyed wintering at Swiss resorts, where excellent skating conditions were virtually guaranteed for several months. With six hours of daily skating,[6] it is no wonder that he became quite skilled. He was the only person to pass the Big Bear test at Grindelwald in 1902.[7]

Oddly, he does not seem to have competed very much. After registering, but not showing up, for the Holland Challenge Bowl at St. Moritz in 1903[8] and being "obliged by a bad fall to withdraw" from the Skating Bowl at Davos in 1904,[9] he finished third in a field of five skaters at a club competition at Grindelwald.[10] His name is notably absent from the list of champions in James R. Hines, *The English Style: Figure Skat-*

---

5. The National Skating Association is now called British Ice Skating. I am grateful to Elaine Hooper for information from its records.

6. Masters, *The Life of E. F. Benson*, 148.

7. "Grindelwald Skating Club," *The Field* 99, no. 2567 (March 1902): 328.

8. "Skating at St. Moritz: The Holland Challenge Bowl," *The Field* 101, no. 2617 (February 1903): 307.

9. "Skating and Tobagganing at Davos," *The Field* 103, no. 2664 (January 1904): 106.

10. "Grindelwald Skating Club," *The Field* 103, no. 2667 (February 1904): 203.

ing's Oldest Tradition (Westwood, MA: Neponset River Press, 2008) and in the results recorded by British Ice Skating.

Benson's preferred type of skating, the English style, featured an upright body posture with the limbs held still and the knees straight, high speeds, and extremely long edges. He was a strong proponent of this style a time when an alternative, the International style was taking hold. In contrast to the English style, the International style featured short, tight edges, and tricks, like jumps and spins, skated with bent knees and mobile limbs. With the founding of the International Skating Union in 1892, competitions were formalized—in the International style. Skaters who preferred the English style were left out. An article in *The Field* noted that "doubt existed as to whether the programme of the [International Skating] Union was such as would enable British skaters to compete with any chance of success" because "on the Continent very different ideas of 'form' exist from those prevalent in England."[11] The International style is the ancestor of today's skating, but the English style survives at the Guilford Spectrum Leisure Center in Surrey, where members of the Royal Skating Club practice it every summer.[12]

In 1908, the year figure skating (in the International style only) first appeared in the Olympics, Benson's well-known book on skating in the English style[13] was

11. "National Skating Association—Figure Skating Department," *The Field* 82, no. 2132 (November 1893): 697.

12. See http://www.theroyalskatingclub.co.uk/.

13. Benson, *English Figure Skating: A Guide to the Theory and Practice of Skating in the English Style.*

published. The next year, his student, a German skater with the last name Duer, passed the first class test, which the *Field* called "a notable feat for a foreigner in the English style of the strictest school."[14] Masters[15] speculates that he also coached Wilfrid Coleridge.

Benson remained involved in skating and continued writing for the rest of his life. He was a member of the committee for organizing English-style skating competitions in 1930, according to British Ice Skating's records. His last book, an autobiographical work called *Final Edition*, went to his publisher just as he became ill. He died of throat cancer in 1940.[16]

14. "Skating in Switzerland," *The Field* 118, no. 2924 (January 1909): 64.

15. Masters, *The Life of E. F. Benson*, 176.

16. Masters, *The Life of E. F. Benson*, 284-286.

Figure 1: Benson at 22.

Figure 2: Benson at 27.

These Stories

I have selected the stories in this volume based on what they show the reader about skating culture in Benson's time. They include a description of winter in Switzerland for prospective tourists,[17] sketches of life on the ice,[18] tales of society life that feature skating,[19] and descriptions of what awaits unwary vacationers in Switzerland.[20]

The first five stories are set in England, where mild winters made skating rare. The sixth story is not so much a story as a tourist brochure for people considering spending the winter in Switzerland. This was quite popular among avid skaters who, like Benson himself, could afford it, as ice was virtually guaranteed. The last four stories take place in Switzerland, and show how vacationing there could be wonderful, terrifying, or a combination of both. Four of the stories[21] are excerpts from longer works that stand well on their own.

I have left the text of the stories as it was originally published, except for correcting the occasional

---

17. "Winter Pastimes," p. 98.

18. "Skating in Marlborough," p. 18; "The Babe Goes Skating," p. 25, "Mr. Teddy's Skating Skills," p. 38, and "A Comedy of Styles," p. 111.

19. "The Peerage Cure," p. 52 and "How Fear Departed from the Long Gallery," p. 73.

20. "January," p. 126, "The Other Bed," p. 142, and "The Horror-Horn," p. 161.

21. "Skating in Marlborough," p. 18, "The Babe Goes Skating," p. 25, "Mr. Teddy's Skating Skills," p. 38, and "January," p. 126

typo, modernizing the spelling where needed, and enforcing compliance with a consistent style throughout the book.

Skating Stories

Skating in Marlborough

This semi-autobiographical story is one of Benson's first. It's based on the events of his student days at Marlborough College.[22]

Kenwick and I both had got the skating fever. So one evening, when it was just possible that if there was an abnormally hard frost, the ice might bear, we prepared overnight a wholesome, though somewhat chilling breakfast of corned beef and bread and butter, and prepared to start at the Witching hour of 8:20 the following morning for the Forest Pond.

On the morrow, about 8:40 a.m., two figures might have been seen seated on the banks of a lonely far away pond, dubiously frozen. The red frosty sunshine touched the beech trees of Savernake Forest, while to the north stretched away a common of stunted furze bushes, through which, every now and then, came chill blasts of wind which pierced the wanderers to the bone. (You may finish the rest of the description for yourself in the same style.)

Altogether, a less desirable locality in which to breakfast on a cold morning could not have been chosen.

Kenwick was the first to speak: "You may skate on my hands, if you like," said he, "they are far harder frozen than that pond, also larger."

That was evidently a joke, so to make matters pleasant I tried to laugh. But I couldn't do it, I could only

---

22. First published as chapter 4 of *Sketches from Marlborough.*

accentuate the chattering of my teeth. "Anyhow, we'll have breakfast," said I. "I wish we could have brought some tea; it might warm us."

"The burning fiery furnace wouldn't thaw me," said Kenwick.

Reserved silence. Mental survey of position.

"This is a unique situation, I should say," he continued, drawing from his pocket a piece of newspaper, which was folded in an imperfect manner round some scraggy sections of corned beef. He laid it on the ground. "There's the bread and butter somewhere," he continued.

A fuller investigation was rewarded by the discovery of some unhealthy looking bread, cut in substantial slices, with patches of butter distributed in an uneven number over the bilious surface. This was distinctly cheering, and we both felt better.

Another silence ensued, during which the beef vanished more rapidly than the bread and butter, especially the bread. "This is the most outlandish position I have ever been in," said Kenwick, trying to repress a smile; "but doesn't it strike you as being mildly humourous?"

"Very mildly," said I severely, upon which he, so to speak, went out.

"Don't be sick," he said. "You know it was you who proposed coming."

We looked round: between us lay the rapidly diminishing column of corned beef, and the slowly diminishing ditto of bread. The paper it was wrapt in fluttered ominously in the wind. "Like a danger signal," said I.

"Then it would be red," replied Kenwick.

He was certainly getting angry. Before us lay a small piece of water, thinly iced over, "about as big as a pocket-handkerchief," remarked Kenwick, "on which we hope to skate."

"I feel as if I was going to bathe," said I, buckling my ankle-strap.

"Perhaps you are," replied Kenwick, sympathetically. "But I shan't if I find you do."

However, he weighed at least two stone more than I did, and as I told him, he had better go on first, for if I went on first, even if it bore me, it would not necessarily bear him, while if it bore him I might venture to come on without danger. Thus he was the better test.

There was something genuine about this logic, and so Kenwick, after finishing the corned beef, launched himself on to the ice. A terrific sound as of artillery was heard all over the pocket-handkerchief, and the ice bent beneath his feet like the sea in a heavy ground swell. I thought perhaps he would feel more at home if I talked to him, so I stood on the bank and shouted encouragement.

"It's all right if it bends," said I, "it's only if it cracks that—" and here my reply was drowned for a moment by another artillery report.

However, by this time he had gone over most of the surface (and it didn't take long to do that), and so, in a moment of strong physical courage, I buckled my skates and joined him. It certainly was beautiful ice, perfectly clear, with that peculiar satin sort of feeling about it. We saw the weeds at the bottom waving uneasily as we passed over them; also, there was the conviction never absent from us—that at any moment the ice might give way.

Kenwick was practising what he called cross-cuts. I don't quite know what a cross-cut may be, but what Kenwick did was this. He skated up in a rapid and irregular manner to near the bank, and then lifted one foot from the ice in a hesitating way, and made several convulsive movements with his body. The result of this was that his skate said "Gr-r-r-r," and he fell against the bank, upon which he said "Bother, I slipped." Sometimes he said "Dash it," and on those occasions it was a loop. It seems rather an easy figure to do; but when I suggested he should do it in the middle of the pond where there was more room, he declined.

The ice in the middle of the pond looked good, and in a moment of rashness I skated on to it. It is needless to state that it instantly gave way, and landed me, so to speak, in about three feet of water, very cold and rather slimy.

This amused Kenwick very much, and he so far forgot himself as to fall down backwards, full length along the ice. Naturally the ice "chucked," and he got soaked from head to foot. I felt that if I had not been so cold I should also have been extremely amused. After that we went home.

The Babe Goes Skating

In this excerpt from The Babe, BA, colle-
giate adventures continue as the eponymous
hero briefly catches the skating fever.[23]

Where three times slipping from the outside
    edge
I bumped the ice into three several stars.

Tennyson.

The frost continued, black and clean, and the Babe, like the Polar Bear, thought it would be nice to prac- tise skating. He bought himself a pair of Dowler blades with Mount Charles fittings,[24] which he was assured by an enthusiastic friend were the only skates with which it was possible to preserve one's self-respect, and fondly hoped that self-respect was a synonym for bal- ance. Hitherto his accomplishments in this particular line had been limited to what is popularly known as a little outside edge, but Reggie, who was a first-rate skater undertook his education. The Babe, however, refused to leave his work altogether alone, for he was

---

23. First published as chapter 20, "The Babe's Minor Diver- sions," of *The Babe, B.A.: Being the Uneventful History of a Young Gentleman at Cambridge University.*

24. These skates were popular among all but the most expert skaters. Benson recommends Mount Charles fittings—the bits that connect the blade to the boot—but not Dowler blades (*En- glish Figure Skating: A Guide to the Theory and Practice of Skating in the English Style*, 16). See figure 3 on page 21.

beginning to be seriously touched with the sapping epidemic, and he and Reggie used to set off about one, taking lunch with them, to the skating club, of which Reggie was a member, and of which the Babe was not.

Sykes only went with them once, and he would not have gone then, had it been possible to foresee that he would put skates in the same category as croquet balls and bathers, but it was soon clear that he did. He made a bee-line for the unemployed leg of Professor Robertson, who was conscious of having done the counter rocking turn[25] for the first time in his life without the semblance of a scrape, and brought him down like a rabbit shot through the head. The Babe hurried across to the assistance of the disabled scientist, and dragged Sykes away. But Sykes had his principles, and as he dared not use threats to the Babe, he implored, almost commanded him not to put on his skates.

"Sykes, dear, you are a little unreasonable," said the Babe pacifically. "Reggie, what are we to do with Sykes? There was nearly one scientist the less in this naughty world."

The cab in which they had driven up, was still waiting, and at Reggie's suggestion Sykes was put inside and driven back to the stable where he slept.

The Babe wobbled industriously about, trying to skate large, and not deceive himself into thinking that a three was finished as soon as he had made the turn, and Reggie practised by himself round an orange, waiting for a four to be made up,[26] until the Babe ate it.

---

25. A counter in today's skating parlance.

26. Four was the most common number of skaters in a figure

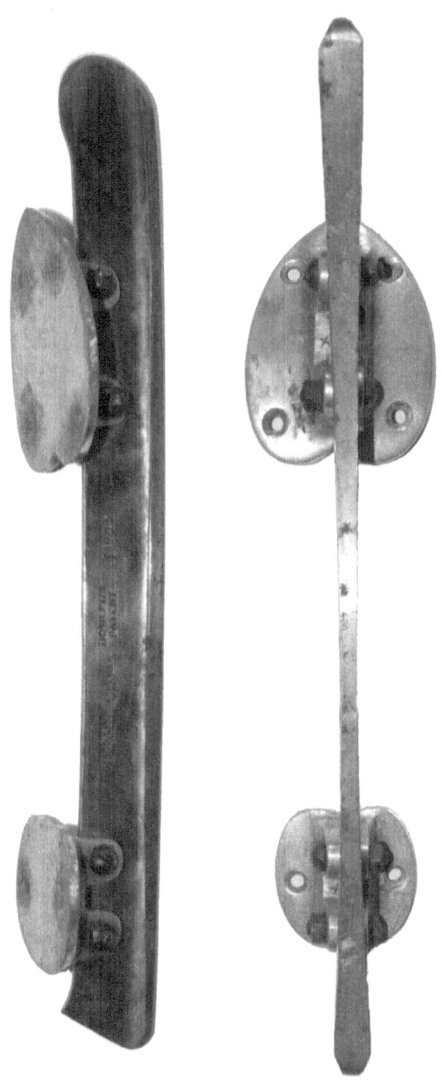

Figure 3: Dowler skates with Mount Charles fastenings. Note how the blade flares out at the ends.

About the third day the Babe was hopelessly down with the skating fever, which went badly with the sapping epidemic. He took his skates round to King's in the evening, after skating all day, for the sapping epidemic was rapidly fleeing from him like a beautiful dream at the awakening, and skated on the fountain; he slid about his carpet trying to get his pose right; he put his looking-glass on the floor and corrected the position of the unemployed foot; he traced grapevines with a fork on the tablecloth and loops with wineglasses; he dreamed that he covered a pond with alternate brackets and rocking turns,[27] and woke up to find it was not true; he even watered the pavement outside his rooms in order to get a little piece of ice big enough for a turn, with the only result that the bed-maker, coming in next morning, fell heavily over it, barking her elbow, and breaking the greater part of the china she was carrying, which, as the Babe said, was happily not his. Unfortunately, however, the porter discovered it, as he brought round letters, and ruthlessly spread salt thickly over it, while the baffled Babe looked angrily on from the window.

Snow fell after this, and the Babe proposed tobogganing down Market Hill. He talked it over with Reggie, and they quarrelled as to which was the top of the hill and which the bottom, "for it would never do," said the scrupulous Babe, "to be seen tobogganing up hill," and

in English combined skating. An orange was used to mark the center of the figure. The skaters followed the instructions of a caller.

27. Rockers in today's skating parlance.

on referring the matter to a third person, it was decided that the hill was perfectly level, so that they were both right and both wrong, whichever way you chose to look at the question.

The King's Comby (which is an abbreviation for Combination and means Junior Combination Room, but takes place in quite a different apartment) went off satisfactorily. The Babe, secure in the knowledge that there was no rhyme to Babe in the English language (his other name, which I have omitted to mention before, was Arbuthnot, and it would require an excess of ingenuity to find a rhyme even to that), made scurrilous allusions, most of them quite unfounded, about his friends, in vile decasyllables, and enjoyed himself very much. Later in the evening he with two of the performers in the original play acted a short skit on the Agamemnon,[28] in which he parodied himself with the most ruthlessly realistic accuracy, and killed Agamemnon in a sponging tin with the aid of a landing net and a pair of scissors. Last of all he disgraced himself by stamping out in the snow, in enormous letters, the initials of a popular and widely known don of the college, with such thoroughness, that the grass has never grown since, and the initials are to be seen to this day, to witness if I lie. The proceedings terminated about three in the morning, and the Babe was left waiting for some minutes outside the porter's lodge at Trinity, while that indignant official got out of bed to open the gate to him.

The Babe ought to have caught a bad cold, but with

---

28. A play by Aeschylus.

an indefensible miscarriage of justice, it was the porter
who caught cold, and not he, and the Babe observed
cynically, when he heard of it, that the memory of the
dog in the nursery rhyme, that bit a man from Islington
in the leg, and then died itself, had at last been avenged.

Christmas, the Babe announced, fell early that year,
and consequently he with several others stayed up till
Christmas Eve, when they were allowed to stay no
longer. He had gone up to town for two days to play in
the University Rugby match, which he had been largely
instrumental in winning, for the ground was like a but-
tered ballroom floor, a state of things which the Babe
for some occult reason delighted in, and for an hour's
space he proceeded to slip and slide and gloom and
glance in a way that seemed to paralyse his opponents,
and resulted in Cambridge winning by two tries and a
dropped goal. The dropped goal was the Babe's doing:
theoretically it had been impossible, for he appeared to
drop it out of the middle of a scrimmage, but it counted
just the same, and he had also secured one of the tries.
The *Sportsman* for December 15th gives a full account
of the match; also the Babe's portrait, in which he looks
like a cross between a forger and a parricide.

On returning to Cambridge, in order to be up to
date, he and some friends went out carol-singing one
night, visiting the heads of colleges, and the houses of
the married fellows. The Babe acted as showman and
spoke broad Somersetshire, which interested a certain
philologist, who had no suspicion that they were not
town people, very much. The Babe declared that his
father and grandfather had lived in Barnwell all their

lives, and that he himself had never even attempted to set foot out of Cambridgeshire except once on the August Bank Holiday, when he had intended to go to Hunstanton but had missed the train. At this point, however, the philologist winked and said: "Mr. Arbuthnot, I believe." They collected in all seventeen shillings and eightpence, which they settled should be given to a local charity, but the Babe, as he counted the amount over with trembling, avaricious fingers, looked up with a brilliant smile as he announced the total and exclaimed: "Not a penny of that shall the poor ever see." They also got what Rudyard Kipling calls "lashings of beer" at several houses, and Bill Sykes, who had been coached to carry a small tin into which offerings of money were put by the open-handed householder, was without a shadow of reason filled with so uncontrollable a fit of rage at the sight of the cook at one of the houses in Selwyn Gardens, who patted him on the head, and called him a pretty dear, that he dropped the tin mug, and nipped her shrewdly in the parts about the ankle.

Reggie parted from the Babe at the station, the latter going to London, and Reggie to Lincolnshire. The Babe travelled first because he said Sykes refused to go second or third, but that intelligent animal, poking his nose out from under the seat just as the guard was taking the tickets, was ignominiously hauled out, and compelled to go in the van, which cannot be considered as a class at all.

Mr. Teddy's Skating Skills

This excerpt from one of Benson's novels depicts the pride skaters have in their skills and how they respond when it is shot down. Many of today's adult skaters can sympathize with Mr. Teddy as he finds himself shown up by youngsters.[29]

The clear cold weather held on its wintry course, and was behaving precisely as if Charles Dickens had been promoted to the post of chief clerk. There were a couple of days of heavy snow, and on the top of that set in a determined black frost, which speedily covered with ever-thickening ice the big lake down by the river. It was but natural that a place so given over to athletic activities as Lambton should have a skating-club, of which, quite as naturally, Teddy was organizing secretary and chief executant. This skating-club in the ordinary tropical English winter lay dormant, warmly hibernating, but as soon as a good frost set in, its members briskly paid up their five-shilling subscriptions, and hired a good piece of ice, which was roped off from the rest of the lake and formed their club-rink, where those who had passed a certain easy test to the satisfaction of Teddy and Mrs. Joyce could practise unimpeded by the merely progressive crowd who joined hands. One

---

29. First published in *Mr. Teddy* (London: T. Fisher Unwin, Ltd., 1917), 224–237 in the UK and *The Tortoise* (New York: George H. Doran Company, 1917), 200–211 in the US.

glad morning came the word that the lake was safe for
skaters, and Teddy, starving for the rare sport, hurried
off before Robin had so much as appeared at breakfast,
to see that the sacred place was duly roped off, and to
practise the figures at which he was so pre-eminent. He
could do a three on either foot, he could make complete circles of outside edge forwards and backwards,
and could lay down a serpentine line of outside and
inside edge alternately with the help of waving of the
unemployed leg, which was considered to be the near-
est approach to perpetual motion ever beheld, for he
could go on serpentining away round and round the lake
till mere fatigue terminated his progress. Otherwise it
seemed that he would never stop. Also there was an
amazing manoeuvre called a rocker, which Teddy and
Mrs. Joyce considered to be far the most difficult feat
that could reasonably be supposed to be within the
reach of themselves or other members of the club. It
entailed starting on an outside edge, and then by a sudden and simultaneous release of arms and the other leg
turning on to the outside edge backwards. Only Teddy
and Mrs. Joyce could do it at all (and they not much),
but when it was seen that either of them was doing
rockers, other skaters stopped and with eager eyes beheld the realization of their wildest dreams. Another
treat was to see Mr. Teddy and Mrs. Joyce skate a
combined figure together with an orange for a centre.
They changed edges and turned threes simultaneously
in obedience to Teddy's calls, and certainly made a very
great deal out of slender materials.

Teddy found a wonderful sheet of black ice, and being the first arrival had the opportunity to steady himself on his edges before others came. Modest as he was, he could not but enjoy so unequalled a pre-eminence as he held in this delightful sport, and he had soon laid down a quantity of threes on each foot and an almost endless serpentine line. By degrees the surface of the club-rink began to be dotted with members, and, on the unreserved part outside, he saw Marion, who enjoyed skating very much, and even left her work for it, but could not be considered very proficient. She gave a great scoop on to the ice with one foot, and then putting both feet together let this impulse exhaust itself, while she glared with fixed and truculent eyes at anybody who came too near her. When she stopped, she scooped again, and again slid forward. But what most of all she liked was to get some proficient friend to skate with her. Then her forbidding countenance became wreathed in smiles, and clutching her victim's arm with talons of iron she was trundled round the pond without the need of scooping at all. She said that to get Mr. Teddy to perform this office for her was to enjoy the sensation of flying. She was not sufficiently at ease to talk while this was going on, but she smiled incessantly, and occasionally, leaning more on her escort, lifted one of her feet from the ice and immediately replaced it, lurching heavily.

Teddy's feet were tingling for his rockers, but he continued to give Miss Marion the sensation of flying until she told him that she had flown enough for the present and would enjoy the sensation of sitting down. So leaving her, he skated to the end of the lake where was the club-rink, with his head thrown back, and his hands clasped negligently behind him (just as if he was doing nothing at all), entirely on the outside edge, first one foot and then the other. Then, still cursorily, he cut a three on the right foot, and took up a back edge, and varied his performance by executing a piece of the famous serpentine line. It was impossible to acquit him of gusto in the studied nonchalance of his progress: here was he doing, as he sauntered along, all the feats to attain which others spent hours of persevering practice.

Teddy had not seen either Robin or Rosemary yet, and went swinging along, skating backwards, rather hoping in the deepest recesses of his mind that they had come down and were observing, like the rest of Lambton, his easy and majestic progress. The ice was of that satiny texture that is so flattering to the edges, and he really surprised himself by the firmness with which he went this way and that in bold circles at least three yards long each.

He was now close up to the rope that separated the holy place from the rest of the ice, when close behind him he heard the sharp clatter of some one evidently running on skates within the sacred enclosure, a thing that was quite contrary to all custom in that classical spot. Turning round he saw with some little annoyance that Rosemary was tearing round the edge of the en-closure, just running on her skates, while close behind her followed Robin, doing the same. This would not do at all, for, in the first place, neither of them had passed the test which admitted them inside, and, in the sec-ond, running like that on your skates was the sort of

hooligan proceeding which was only worthy of the un-
enclosed area where the vulgar populace joined hands
and waved sticks. As they raced by him, he could not
but notice how much at home they seemed on their
blades, and he himself would not have cared to go such
a pace. Then as they receded up the edge of the enclosure, he heard Robin shout out, "What is it this time,
Rosemary?" and she screamed back at him, "Outside
rocker." Teddy frowned to himself at this unseemliness,
and then suddenly his pleasant face cleared again. No
doubt Daisy, who was watching them, had let slip the
fact that both he and Mrs. Joyce could do rockers, and
they, having observed his approach, were chaffing him,
and, not knowing at all what a rocker was, were chasing
each other round the ice, and calling their performance
by that hallowed name.

Then suddenly Rosemary ceased running on her
skates, and at top-speed sailed out, with skirts blown
close to her, to the centre of the ice, where Mrs. Joyce
had already put the orange that was the focus of the
combined figure. She was moving at a really tremendous pace, on the outside forward edge, up-right in carriage, and leaning a little back. Just as she got to the
orange, she seemed to Teddy to give an infinitesimal
flick with her lithe loose shoulders, and she was sail-
ing away towards the circumference of the enclosure
again on an indubitable outside back edge. Certainly
she appeared to have performed a rocker, but how had
it happened, for nobody, as far as Teddy knew, could do
a rocker except slowly and with a large kick? The next
moment a wild scream went up, and Robin, no doubt

with the same exalted intention, took the most impe-
rial of falls, with arms and legs wildly flying, and his
agonized scream terminating in a great shout of laughter. Rosemary had caught sight of Teddy, and drew up
with a whiff of scraped ice within a yard of him.

"Oh, Teddy, there you are," she said. "I never dreamed there would be skating till Miss Daisy rang me up.
And you're a frightful swell, I hear. Come and do some
big turns! Oh, look at Robin! Did you ever see such a
gorgeous toss? Oh, and will you and Mrs. Joyce see if
we can qualify for the skating-club? What have we got
to do?"

Teddy's face assumed a reverential expression.

"Rosemary, was that really a rocker you did?" he
asked.

"Yes, it was meant for one. But rather wobbly,
wasn't it? Come and show me. Oh, look, there's Robin
having another shot."

Robin cantered round the edge and launched himself
into the middle of the ice. He, like Rosemary, stood
quiet and upright till he came near the centre, then he
gave that same little flick of his shoulders and away he
sped on the back edge, in a huge smooth curve that
brought him up to where the other two were standing.

"Lord, I thought I should never find my skates," he
said. "I haven't worn them since I was in Switzerland
two winters ago. Teddy, you beast, why didn't you tell
me that there was a chance of skating last night? I'd
have had them ready. Let's have a combined. They say

you're absolutely top-hole. Will you call? Don't make it too hard. Oh, I forgot: Rosemary and I have got to pass our test first, haven't we?"

Teddy thought this would be the best plan, and pulling himself together, though with an odd sinking of the heart, he went off to find Mrs. Joyce to assist him in the work of judging the competitors. She was at the far end of the enclosure, and he progressed there on the famous serpentine line. Robin and Rosemary remained behind, and they looked at each other.

"But what's that?" said Rosemary in a whisper.

"Dunno. Lambton figure. What are we to do? I said I heard he was top-hole."

"So did I. Look, he's doing a three. Oh, Robin! What a three! He hasn't the vaguest notion."

Robin pulled his mouth into gravity.

"I bet you he won't mind a bit," he said. "Look at his skates, too: those things with snaps to them or a key or something. The sort that come off."

Teddy took just as long "not to mind a bit" as it took him and Mrs. Joyce to pass the two candidates. But it did take him that amount of time, for here was he, the acknowledged champion of Lambton, who an hour ago had come regally down into his frozen kingdom and two minutes ago had been hoping that Robin and Rosemary had arrived and were watching his back-edges, suddenly relegated not into the second rank, but into no rank at all. He had been accustomed when candidates came before him to see whether they were up to the standard, to relieve them by kindly encouragement from their natural nervousness, and to skate a three for them to show them to what heights they might rise if they persevered. These threes were at least two yards long both before and after the cusp, and were considered miracles of dashing performance. But now when Rosemary was asked to skate a three, she clattered with her feet on the ice to get up speed, and sailed from end to end of the enclosure, and when Robin was asked to change his edge, instead of kicking in the air with his other foot, in the orthodox Teddy-manner, he appeared merely to look to the left instead of the right, and, lo, his curve to the right slid into a curve to the left. Then when this farce—for so Teddy felt it to be—of judging two candidates who were out of sight, in point of proficiency, of their judges, was over, they discreetly retired while Mrs. Joyce and Teddy considered the merits of their performance.

"I'm not sure that I altogether approve of their style," said Mrs. Joyce. "Do you, Mr. Teddy? It's so hard to tell what they are doing. Now when you change your edge it's easy to see what you are about. I daresay if you showed them once or twice how you do it—"

Teddy laughed.

"My dear lady," he said, "that I entirely refuse to do. We must take it joyfully: they can skate and we can't. That's where we are. But I'm going to learn, if I break every bone in my body."

"Well, if you insist on passing them," she said.

"For my part, I really do. Dear me, the idea of a skater like me standing gravely by, to see if Miss Rosemary can do a three on each foot!"

Mrs. Joyce was disposed still to cling to her disdain.

"I expect they'll be very unsteady when they skate combined figures with us," she said.

Teddy had an exceedingly trying hour after this. He placed himself straight away under the tuition of Rosemary, who, after putting her late judge through his paces, broke to him the fact that he must begin again from the very beginning, and forget all that he had thought he could do. Teddy, whose rockers had been watched by the skating-club with an admiration in which envy had really no place, so far were they removed from the attainable ambitions, found that not only must he learn rockers again, but long before he arrived at that point he must learn how to skate edges, and before he learned to skate edges, must learn how to strike. It was better, so he unerringly inferred, to know nothing than to know what he knew, and, with set face and determination gleaming in his kindly eyes, he, the champion of winter sports, became a tyro, and in the eyes of Mrs. Vickary, who came down to look on, not only a tyro but a charlatan. She found a seat next Daisy, and proceeded to poison the frosty air.

"Well, I'm sure I am very much surprised at all this," she said. "To think that all these years we have thought that dear Mr. Teddy was such a wonderful skater, and now to find out that he can't skate at all. Look at him trying to imitate Mr. Robin! Is it not quite laughable? And poor Mrs. Joyce, too! Upon my word this is a come-down for them. What a pity that people give out that they can do things of which they have no idea. It is like Mr. Winkle over again, is it not?"

Depreciation of other people was Mrs. Vickary's

method of ingratiating herself, and her acid remarks were really meant to show how much she appreciated Daisy's having retired from her post of solo-singer. She had been ousted (Mrs. Vickary had begun to think that her own diplomacy had been somehow and inexplicably responsible for this), and she would probably like to find that others had been ousted too. "Or is it naughty of me to compare our dear Mr. Teddy to Mr. Winkle?" she went on. "But do you not remember the scene where Mr. Winkle said he could skate? Ah! Mr. Teddy has fallen down! I do hope he has not hurt himself. Dear me, what a good thing Miss Marion is not here! I am sure she would say some dreadfully unkind, sarcastic thing. But she is not permitted to come into this sacred enclosure, is she? She does not rise to dear Mr. Teddy's standard of what skating should be. But we shall have to alter all our ideas now!"

Out of the corner of her eye Daisy perceived that Marion was stealthily sliding towards them, catching hold of seats by the edge of the ice or of anybody who happened to be handy. By rule, she was not allowed on this part of the ice at all, as Mrs. Vickary had said, but then Marion always did exactly as she chose. Daisy waited till she was quite close up to them, simmering with indignation. Then she turned sharply round.

"Oh, there you are, Marion!" she said. "We were talking of you and of this skating revolution. Mrs. Vickary said you would be sure to be very unkind and sarcastic about it."

Marion anchored herself quite firmly between Daisy and a chair, clutching hold of each of them. Then she gave a grim nod to Mrs. Vickary.

"Skating revolution?" she said. "What's happened?"

"Only that we have all found that Miss Rosemary and Mr. Robin skate a million times better than anybody else. And so Mr. Teddy is beginning to learn it all from the beginning. There he is!"

"I call that sporting," answered Marion. "That's my idea of being sporting."

Mrs. Vickary gave a little titter. "There! Did I not say she would be sarcastic?" she said.

"Then you are most uncommonly mistaken," said Marion.

After which awful speech, the chair she was holding on to slid away, and she fell on her back. But even as she lay on the ice she repeated: "Thoroughly sportsmanlike. Pull me up, Daisy. How I adore skating."

When she got to her feet, Mrs. Vickary was titupping away in her thrush-like manner.

"Vickary!" said Marion, in a voice of withering scorn, without further comment.

Just as in the matter of the solo-singing, then, so in these skating matters, the banner of youth was suddenly hoisted over the mediaeval and familiar fortresses. In itself it was a wholly trivial affair whether Daisy sang solos or her place was taken by Rosemary, even as it was trivial whether Teddy was the champion of the skating world or was relegated to the position of humblest learner. But what lay below the surface was the "Dammerung" of the older generation, the heed-

less, inevitable supplanting of it by the new. In themselves such things mattered no more than the actual
fall of the barometer-needle; it was what they stood for,
what they indicated and prophesied, that should be of
concern. And yet the analogy hardly holds, for these
rain-clouds coming up were such brilliant sunlit spires,
sky-children of breezy weather. There they floated, re-
joicing in the upper air, bringing with them gladness
wherever they moved as well as the shadows that they
inevitably cast, which, in a manner of speaking, were
wholly independent of them. By their very nature, the
nature of their age, they cast shadow, and by the same
nature diffused light. There was no stopping or staying
them anyhow; it was for the inhabitants of the plain
below but to observe them, to wonder what they were
going to do. Dazzled by the brightness, Teddy looked
at one of them; it was as if he was putting up a ladder
into the sky, and walking up it rung by rung.

"I want; I want," he said, and still mounted.

But he began to wonder what the clouds were saying
to each other.

The Peerage Cure

In this charming story, audacious social climber Amy Bondham uses skating to advance her position. Her experience highlights the dangers of natural ice.[30]

It had been the most wonderful autumn for Mrs. Amy Bondham: never before had she lived so exclusively in the society of the great and the ennobled. She had spent October in a round (you might call it a merry-go-round) of visits; for though she had originally planned only four week-ends, she had made herself so popular at each of them that some member of the party had insisted, or at least consented, that she should spend the intervening days before her next engagement at a Castle or a Grange or something very moated and hereditary. Then, when the world began to stream back to London again in November, it was her turn, and every day the hospitable table in her house in Mount Street was laid for intimate and high-born little parties. Though still fond of professional distinction, she had dropped, but only temporarily, her literary, artistic, and histrionic friends, whom she meant to pick up again in the close time for the high-born circle which flocked to the Riviera after Christmas.

Just now her aim and ambition was the high-born, and the pages of her "Peerage," in which she put a lit-

---

30. First published as "The Peerage Cure," *The Windsor Magazine* 64, no. 379 (July 1926): 119–124.

tle cross in the margin opposite the names of those who had entertained her or been entertained by her, became full of these discreet little pencil-marks, and pleasantly swollen became the album of picture postcards into which she gummed, with absolutely scrupulous honesty, only the photographs of mansions which she had actually visited, inscribed with the appropriate date. The rumour, therefore, that she bought these in indiscriminate packets, as illustrating the houses at which she would like to stay, was an unfounded fabrication, devised by the jealousy of less fortunate competitors.

Her circular and devoted little husband Christopher had accompanied her on her progress in October, but he was not so strong as she, and also was quite unable to resist the pleasures of the table. Throughout November, in spite of the obedient walks he took daily round and round the park, he remained very liverish and gouty; and when, early in December, Amy was about to set forth on the visit which really was the crown of all her social attainments, he was persuaded by her to go off to Bath, and try to get fit again for the Christmas Campaign. This crowning visit was to the Duke of Whitby, and though it was certainly now coming off, it had required all Amy's tact and perseverance to effect it, for the Duchess had continued to be impervious to her hints for an unusually long time. But finally doggedness carried the day, the Duchess had yielded, and had asked her to Doncaster Castle while she was entertaining a bevy of distinguished savants from the Psychological Conference in York. It was not precisely the sort of party which Amy would have chosen, but if it had been a party of chimney-sweeps and chiropodists she would have eagerly accepted. She could murmur her "Nunc Dimittis"[31] now, and see about all the clever people she had dropped.

She and Christopher dined alone for the first time since September, as Amy delightedly remembered, on the evening before he went to Bath and she to Doncaster. For once she had broken her rule about the picture-postcard album, and had allowed herself to buy four striking views of the magnificent Norman pile in which she would be dining next night, and subsequently sleeping, if excitement would allow her to do so.

"I may as well put them in now," she said, "because they will just fill up the last page in my book. I must get a new one when I come back, for we're going to Eagles for Christmas and Tenterden Grange for the New Year."

"Better not, Posie," he said. "It may bring bad luck. The Duchess may put you off to-morrow morning. You've not got there yet."

She laughed.

"You superstitious old man!" she said. "That's gout. It's just acidity. Morbid ideas like that are purely physical.—Where's the gum-pot?—My dear, what a wonderful autumn it has been. Look, the book was nearly new in September."

She turned over the rich pages.

"All those!" she said. "I think I shall have it bound in a manner more worthy of its contents. I wonder what we shall have in the next volume?"

---

31. Literally "now you dismiss," this refers to the Song of Simeon.

She came and sat on the hearth-rug, propped her back against the arm of his chair, and stretched her feet out to the blaze.

"Perhaps there won't be a next volume," she said, "for really, Christopher, I feel I've been very frivolous all the autumn."

The words "perhaps there won't be a next" gave Christopher a queer little shudder, but that probably was acidity too.

"You bet there will, Posie," he said, "if there are enough fine houses left in England to fill it. You have become a fashionable little dame."

She sighed.

"But there are other things besides that," she said, rather doubtfully. "There's that volume of Proust which I must read, and *The Life and Times of Tutankhamen*, and that book on Auto-suggestion. I shall take them up to Yorkshire. And when my visit's over I shall join you at Bath."

"Better not do that," he said. "You'll be bored to death."

She considered.

"Well, we'll see," she said. " I've noticed sometimes in the paper that there are interesting people at Bath and some interesting houses in the neighbourhood," she added.

There had been a week's frost in England, and Amy, next morning, seeing in the paper that there was skating in the north, decided to take her skates with her. She was quite an expert on the ice, having spent the last winter at St. Moritz,[32] where she had come across a great many agreeable people, and had, in fact, laid the foundation of the superb autumn she had just enjoyed. One of her picture postcards also showed a lake below the walls of the Castle, and another a mediaeval moat round it. Probably the lake or the moat would bear, and the idea of discussing the newest views on Autosuggestion with eminent psychologists, and then breaking off to astonish them by her lissome feats on the ice, was very attractive. Like most of her plans this turned out well, for the Duke was an ardent skater himself, and after opening the Psychological Conference with a weighty speech, he refused to attend any more meetings, and stopped at home in order to waltz with Amy on the ice-covered moat. His secretary was an adequate pianist, and he was bidden to neglect all his business and play dance music for them. Wrapped in a fur coat, this unfortunate young man sat by the open window of the pink drawing-room so that the lively strains might reach the dancers, while Amy and the Duke pirouetted all day on the frozen water of the moat immediately below. One evening a Royal Princess dined at the Castle, and Amy grew greater than ever, for they skated again after dinner, and she nestled against the Riband of the Garter. She sat up half the night writing one account of all this to poor Christopher at Bath and another to a struggling young friend of hers who wrote paragraphs for the Press. She would make half a dozen paragraphs

---

32. One of the Swiss resorts favored by English skaters.

out of such material, and Amy, though yawning her head off, did not go to bed till she had fully completed this act of disinterested kindness.

The day of her departure, already twice postponed, arrived, and the pain of parting was slightly lessened by the fact that a thaw had set in. The Duke, however, said that the ice would hold for the morning, and they swished about in ever-deepening puddles of water. Ominous crackings and bubblings of air at last warned them that the ice was safe no longer, but then it was too late. A piece collapsed, and they were left standing in thick mud with icy cold water about up to the waist.

They struggled out, and Amy, after a change and a hot bath, protested that she never caught cold, and was none the worse. She was urged to postpone her departure again, but Christopher must not be disappointed once more, for she was to join him at Bath next day, since the papers announced the arrival there of some interesting people. But she had a bad shivering fit on the way up to London, and it was evident that she had broken her rule for once and caught a severe chill. She was well enough next day to write an amazing quantity of postcards to her friends, asking them all to come and see her, but not well enough to travel. The day after she was not well enough to do anything at all except to have a high temperature, and all the friends had to be put off.

She grew rapidly worse: pleurisy set in. She became slightly delirious and babbled in a way that puzzled her nurse about garters and strawberry-leaves. It was in vain that she was assured that her garters were quite

Figure 4: "Wrapped in a fur coat, this unfortunate young man sat by the open window of the pink drawing-room so that the lively strains might reach the dancers."

safe, and when her nurse told her that strawberries were out of season, she said drowsily, "Yes, but strawberry-leaves aren't." In the intervals of delirium, though her breathing was difficult, she seemed extraordinarily content and happy.

Then pleuro-pneumonia developed, and Christopher was sent for. It was not a very severe attack, but there were disquieting symptoms. She made no effort of any kind to fight and resist: she seemed like one who had attained the goal of earthly ambition, and had no desire left for the accomplishment of which she had the will to live.

"I don't like that symptom," said the doctor to Christopher after one of his visits. "The state of her lungs is not such as to warrant our taking—well, a serious view of her condition, though of course pneumonia is always anxious work. Her strength is well maintained, her heart action is quite good, but she must somehow be roused. Go in and sit with her, and try to interest her in things which used to interest her. She mustn't talk, but you try subject after subject, and see if you can't get her to rouse herself."

He shook hands.

"I shall be back about two o'clock," he said. "You mustn't be too anxious yet. She has plenty of vitality if we can only get it to work."

Christopher went to her room. She was lying quite still, her eyes sometimes open, sometimes shut. She knew him, and smiled faintly.

"Now I've come to sit with you a bit," he said. "How

do you feel, darling? You mustn't talk, you know; better not to talk. I'll do all the talking. Perhaps you'd like me to read to you."

She seemed drowsy and very apathetic, but her eyes grew a little more alive at this suggestion.

"Yes, read," she whispered. "Good Christopher."

On the table at the foot of her bed were the book by Proust and the new work on Auto-suggestion.

"Ah, I know what you would like," he said. "Something out of that book of Proust's which you took to Doncaster with you. Will you give me that book, nurse? Very interesting, I am sure."

The invalid's face grew fretful.

"No, not that stupid rubbish," she whispered.

"Well, shall we try that book on Auto-suggestion, dear?" said Christopher. "You were very much interested in that. You told me you were going to read it in the train."

Her forehead furrowed itself into unhappy creases.

"Boring nonsense," she said. "How stupid you all are."

Christopher tried the effect of telling her about Bath, but she took not the smallest interest in Bath. He told her how the telephone-bell had been ringing: everyone who knew she was not well had been inquiring after her, and everyone who didn't know had been asking her to dinner. That uncreased her forehead a little, but still she did not seem to care much, and poor Christopher's heart sank. He realised then what a change there was.

He racked his brains for something more. He felt wretchedly helpless, and the waters of Bath had not purged the acidity from him to such an extent that he could think without superstitious forebodings about those picture postcards of Doncaster Castle.

She gave a little sob.

"No, not Marquises," she said. "Not Marquises. Garters and strawberry-leaves."

The nurse had come to the bedside, and was looking anxiously at her. "That's what she kept saying night and day," she said. "I told her that her garters were all right and it wasn't the season for strawberries, and I suppose she got tired of trying to make me understand. And now she's begun again. Whatever can she mean?"

"Garters and strawberry-leaves," said Amy faintly.

Christopher crushed his temples in his hands. Some remote association, dim as yet, began to form itself in his mind. It was connected somehow with something Amy had written to him in one of those wonderful letters from Doncaster.

"Your garters, darling?" he said.

"No, his," said Amy.

"She's wandering," said the nurse, shaking down a clinical thermometer. "I hope her temperature isn't going up again."

Suddenly Christopher sprang up.

"No, she's not wandering," he cried. "Oh, why did nobody tell me sooner? I know the sort of thing she means, and we'll get at it. She wanted me to read, too."

He bent over her.

"About the Duke of Whitby, isn't it, dear?" he asked.

A faint flush came on her pallid cheeks.

"Yes, all about him," she whispered.

Christopher gave a little squeal of triumph, and ran from the room.

Figure 5: "Christopher gave a little squeal of triumph, and ran from the room."

Figure 6: "A faint flush came on her pallid cheeks."

He tore downstairs without a thought of his twinging toe, and came rushing up again, three steps at a time, with her copy of the "Peerage." He turned rapidly over the leaves with their copious little pencil-marks, until he came to W, and sat down again by her bed, and read.

"Whitby, Duke of. James Francis Adelbert Charlemayne de Vere, K.G., K.C.M.G., K.C.B., O.M., P.C. Born 1882. Educated at Eton and Christ Church College, Oxford. Late Major in 1st Life Guards, Knight of the Order of the Holy Roman Empire, of the Golden Fleece. Married in 1906."

A happy little sigh came from the bed.

"Ah, that's nice," said Amy, in stronger tones. "Go on."

"Married in 1906," continued Christopher, "Frances Elizabeth Plantagenetta, second daughter of 5th Duke of Merionethshire, and has issue: John James Plantagenet, Marquis of Pateley, born 1908; Lady Cynthia Elizabeth Plantagenetta, born 1909. Aunts living— Would you like to hear about the Aunts, darling?"

Amy turned her face towards him.

"Yes, all," she whispered, "and the collaterals. And when you've finished them go on to the Merionethshires."

Christopher read and read and read. There was no end of Whitby collaterals, and the Merionethshires seemed as the sand of the sea for number. But life was coming back to Amy, her breathing grew less distressed, her temperature declined. Half an hour's solid information about these noble lines was poured out in Christopher's sympathetic voice, and she seemed to grow stronger every moment.

At last it was all done.

"I shall get better now," she said. "It was just that I wanted, and nobody would understand. Christopher, you've saved me. I feel hungry, too; I should like a little chicken-broth, and then I think I shall have a nap. Tell everyone I am better and shall soon be well. So happy again!"

Dr. Elliott came back at about two o'clock, as he had promised. Amy was sunk in a peaceful, restorative sleep and was smiling as she slumbered. A glance at her and a couple of words with the nurse was enough for the professional eye, and he came downstairs again to Christopher rubbing his hands.

"Well, that's all right," he said. "You've done the trick, Mr. Bondham. A marked change for the better, and I may say she's turned the corner. How did you manage to rouse her to interest in life again?"

"I read to her a little," said Christopher modestly.

How Fear Departed from the Long Gallery

Today's skaters will relate well to the one in this spook story, who is forced to stay off the ice while recovering from an injury. Recovery has perils of its own.[33]

Church-Peveril is a house so beset and frequented by spectres, both visible and audible, that none of the family which it shelters under its acre and a half of green copper roofs takes psychical phenomena with any seriousness, for to the Peverils the appearance of a ghost is a matter of hardly greater significance than is the appearance of the post to those who live in more ordinary houses. It arrives, that is to say, practically every day, it knocks (or makes other noises), it is observed coming up the drive (or in other places). I myself, when staying there have seen the present Mrs. Peveril, who is rather short sighted, peer into the dusk, while we were taking our coffee on the terrace after dinner, and say to her daughter:

"My dear, was not that the Blue Lady who has just gone into the shrubbery. I hope she won't frighten Flo. Whistle for Flo, dear."

(Flo, it may be remarked, is the youngest and most precious of many dachshunds.)

---

33. From *The Room in the Tower and Other Stories*, 2nd edition (London: Mills and Boon, 1912).

Blanche Peveril gave a cursory whistle, and crunched the sugar left unmelted at the bottom of her coffee-cup between her very white teeth.

"Oh, darling, Flo isn't so silly as to mind," she said. "Poor blue Aunt Barbara is such a bore! Whenever I meet her she always looks as if she wanted to speak to me, but when I say, 'What is it, Aunt Barbara?' she never utters, but only points somewhere towards the house, which is so vague. I believe there was something she wanted to confess about two hundred years ago, but she has forgotten what it is."

Here Flo gave two or three short pleased barks, and came out of the shrubbery wagging her tail, and capering round what appeared to me to be a perfectly empty space on the lawn.

"There! Flo has made friends with her," said Mrs. Peveril. "I wonder why she dresses in that very stupid shade of blue."

From this it may be gathered that even with regard to psychical phenomena there is some truth in the proverb that speaks of familiarity. But the Peverils do not exactly treat their ghosts with contempt, since most of that delightful family never despised anybody except such people as avowedly did not care for hunting or shooting, or golf or skating. And as all of their ghosts are of their family, it seems reasonable to suppose that they all, even the poor Blue Lady, excelled at one time in field-sports. So far then they harbour no such unkindness or contempt, but only pity. Of one Peveril, indeed, who broke his neck in vainly attempting to ride up the main staircase on a thoroughbred mare after some monstrous and violent deed in the back-garden, they are very fond, and Blanche comes downstairs in the morning with an eye unusually bright when she can announce that Master Anthony was "very loud" last night. He (apart from the fact of his having been so foul a ruffian) was a tremendous fellow across country, and they like these indications of the continuance of his superb vitality. In fact, it is supposed to be a compliment, when you go to stay at Church-Peveril, to be assigned a bedroom which is frequented by defunct members of the family. It means that you are worthy to look on the august and villainous dead, and you will find yourself shown into some vaulted or tapestried chamber, without benefit of electric light, and are told that great-great-grandmamma Bridget occasionally has vague business by the fireplace, but it is better not to talk to her, and that you will hear Master Anthony "awfully well" if he attempts the front staircase any time before morning. There you are left for your night's repose, and, having quakingly undressed, begin reluctantly to put out your candles. It is draughty in these great chambers, and the solemn tapestry swings and bellows and subsides, and the firelight dances on the forms of huntsmen and warriors and stern pursuits. Then you climb into your bed, a bed so huge that you feel as if the desert of Sahara was spread for you, and pray, like the mariners who sailed with St. Paul, for day. And, all the time, you are aware that Freddy and Harry and Blanche and possibly even Mrs. Peveril are quite capable of dressing up and making disquieting tappings outside your door, so that when you open it some inconjecturable horror fronts you. For myself, I stick steadily to the assertion that I have an obscure valvular disease of the heart, and so sleep undisturbed in the new wing of the house where Aunt Barbara, and great-great-grandmamma Bridget and Master Anthony never pentrate. I forget the details of great-great-grandmamma Bridget, but she certainly cut the throat of some distant relation before she disembowelled herself with the axe that had been used at Agincourt. Before that she had led a very sultry life, crammed with amazing incident.

But there is one ghost at Church-Peveril at which the family never laugh, in which they feel no friendly and amused interest, and of which they only speak just as much as is necessary for the safety of their guests. More properly it should be described as two ghosts, for the "haunt" in question is that of two very young children, who were twins. These, not without reason, the family take very seriously indeed. The story of them, as told me by Mrs. Peveril, is as follows:

In the year 1602, the same being the last of Queen Elizabeth's reign, a certain Dick Peveril was greatly in favour at Court. He was brother to Master Joseph Peveril, then owner of the family house and lands, who two years previously, at the respectable age of seventy-four, became father of twin boys, first-born of his progeny. It is known that the royal and ancient virgin had said to handsome Dick, who was nearly forty years his brother's junior, "'Tis pity that you are not master of Church Peveril," and these words probably suggested to him a sinister design. Be that as it may, handsome Dick, who very adequately sustained the family reputation for wickedness, set off to ride down to Yorkshire, and found that, very conveniently, his brother Joseph had just been seized with an apoplexy, which appeared to be the result of a continued spell of hot weather combined with the necessity of quenching his thirst with an augmented amount of sack, and had actually died while handsome Dick, with God knows what thoughts in his mind, was journeying northwards. Thus it came about that he arrived at Church-Peveril just in time for his brother's funeral. It was with great propriety that he at tended the obsequies, and returned to spend a sympathetic day or two of mourning with his widowed sister-in-law, who was but a faint-hearted dame, little fit to be mated with such hawks as these. On the second night of his stay, he did that which the Peverils regret to this day. He entered the room where the twins slept with their nurse, and quietly strangled the latter as she slept. Then he took the twins and put them into the fire which warms the long gallery. The weather, which up to the day of Joseph's death had been so hot, had changed suddenly to bitter cold, and the fire was heaped high with burning logs and was exultant with flame. In the core of this conflagration he struck out a cremation-chamber, and into that he threw the two children, stamping them down with his riding-boots. They could just walk, but they could not walk out of that ardent place. It is said that he laughed as he added more logs. Thus he became master of Church Peveril.

The crime was never brought home to him, but he lived no longer than a year in the enjoyment of his blood-stained inheritance.   When he lay a-dying he made his confession to the priest who attended him, but his spirit struggled forth from its fleshly coil before Absolution could be given him.   On that very night there began in Church-Peveril the haunting which to this day is but seldom spoken of by the family, and then only in low tones and with serious mien. For, only an hour or two after handsome Dick's death, one of the servants passing the door of the long gallery heard from within peals of the loud laughter so jovial and yet so sinister, which he had thought would never be heard in the house again. In a moment of that cold courage, which is so nearly akin to mortal terror, he opened the door and entered, expecting to see he knew not what manifestation of him who lay dead in the room below. Instead he saw two little white-robed figures toddling towards him hand in hand across the moon-lit floor.

The watchers in the room below ran upstairs startled by the crash of his fallen body, and found him lying in the grip of some dread convulsion. Just before morning he regained consciousness and told his tale. Then pointing with trembling and ash grey finger towards the door, he screamed aloud, and so fell back dead.

During the next fifty years this strange and terrible legend of the twin-babies became fixed and consolidated. Their appearance, luckily for those who inhabit the house, was exceedingly rare, and during these years they seem to have been seen four or five times only. On each occasion they appeared at night, between sunset and sunrise, always in the same long gallery, and always as two toddling children scarcely able to walk.

And on each occasion the luckless individual who saw them died either speedily or terribly, or with both speed and terror, after the accursed vision had appeared to him. Sometimes he might live for a few months: he was lucky if he died, as did the servant who first saw them, in a few hours. Vastly more awful was the fate of a certain Mrs. Canning, who had the ill-luck to see them in the middle of the next century, or to be quite accurate, in the year 1760. By this time the hours and the place of their appearance were well-known, and, as up till a year ago, visitors were warned not to go between sunset and sunrise into the long gallery.

But Mrs. Canning, a brilliantly clever and beautiful woman, admirer also and friend of the notorious sceptic M. Voltaire, wilfully went and sat night after night, in spite of all protestations, in the haunted place. For four evenings she saw nothing, but on the fifth she had her will, for the door in the middle of the gallery opened, and there came toddling towards her the ill-omened innocent little pair. It seemed that even then she was not frightened, but she thought good, poor wretch, to mock at them, telling them it was time for them to get back into the fire. They gave no word in answer, but turned away from her crying and sobbing. Immediately after they disappeared from her vision and she rustled downstairs to where the family and guests in the house were waiting for her, with the triumphant announcement that she had seen them both, and must needs write to M. Voltaire, saying that she had spoken to spirits made manifest. It would make him laugh. But when some months later the whole news reached him he did not laugh at all.

Mrs. Canning was one of the great beauties of her day, and in the year 1760 she was at the height and zenith of her blossoming. The chief beauty, if it is possible to single out one point where all was so exquisite, lay in the dazzling colour and incomparable brilliance of her complexion. She was now just thirty years of age, but, in spite of the excesses of her life, retained the snow and roses of girlhood, and she courted the bright light of day which other women shunned, for it but showed to greater advantage the splendour of her skin. In consequence she was very considerably dismayed one morning, about a fortnight after her strange experience in the long gallery, to observe on her left cheek an inch or two below her turquoise-coloured eyes, a little greyish patch of skin, about as big as a threepenny piece. It was in vain that she applied her accustomed washes and ungents: vain, too, were the arts of her fardeuse and of her medical adviser. For a week she kept herself secluded, martyring herself with solitude and unaccustomed physics, and for result at the end of the week she had no amelioration to comfort herself with: instead this woeful grey patch had doubled itself in size. Thereafter the nameless disease, whatever it was, developed in new and terrible ways. From the centre of the discoloured place there sprouted forth little lichen-like tendrils of greenish-grey, and another patch appeared on her lower lip. This, too, soon vegetated, and one morning on opening her eyes to the horror of a new day, she found that her vision was strangely blurred. She sprang to her looking-glass, and what she saw caused her to shriek aloud with horror. From under her upper eye-lid a fresh growth had sprung up, mushroom-like, in the night, and its filaments extended downwards, screening the pupil of her eye. Soon after her tongue and throat were attacked: the air passages became obstructed, and death by suffocation was merciful after such suffering.

More terrible yet was the case of a certain Colonel Blantyre who fired at the children with his revolver. What he went through is not to be recorded here.

It is this haunting, then, that the Peverils take quite seriously, and every guest on his arrival in the house is told that the long gallery must not be entered after nightfall on any pretext whatever. By day, however, it is a delightful room and intrinsically merits description, apart from the fact that the due understanding of its geography is necessary for the account that here follows. It is full eighty feet in length, and is lit by a row of six tall windows looking over the gardens at the back of the house. A door communicates with the landing at the top of the main staircase, and about halfway down the gallery in the wall facing the windows is another door communicating with the back staircase and servants' quarters, and thus the gallery forms a constant place of passage for them in going to the rooms on the first landing. It was through this door that the baby-figures came when they appeared to Mrs. Canning, and on several other occasions they have been known to make their entry here, for the room out of which handsome Dick took them lies just beyond at the top of the back stairs. Further on again in the gallery is the fireplace into which he thrust them, and at the far end a large bow-window looks straight down the avenue. Above this fire place there hangs with grim significance a portrait of handsome Dick, in the insolent beauty of early manhood, attributed to Holbein, and a dozen other portraits of great merit face the windows. During the day this is the most frequented sitting-room in the house, for its other visitors never appear there then, nor does it then ever resound with the harsh jovial laugh of handsome Dick, which sometimes, after dark has fallen, is heard by passers-by on the landing outside. But Blanche does not grow bright-eyed when she hears it: she shuts her ears and hastens to put a greater distance between her and the sound of that atrocious mirth.

But during the day the long gallery is frequented by many occupants, and much laughter in no wise sinister or saturnine resounds there. When summer lies hot over the land, those occupants lounge in the deep window seats, and when winter spreads his icy fingers and blows shrilly between his frozen palms, congregate round the fireplace at the far end, and perch, in companies of cheerful chatterers, upon sofa and chair, and chair-back and floor. Often have I sat there on long August evenings up till dressing time, but never have I been there when anyone has seemed disposed to linger over-late without hearing the warning: "It is close on sunset: shall we go?" Later on in the shorter autumn days they often have tea laid there, and sometimes it has happened that, even while merriment was most up-roarious, Mrs. Peveril has suddenly looked out of the window and said, "My dears, it is getting so late: let us finish our nonsense downstairs in the hall." And then for a moment a curious hush always falls on loquacious family and guests alike, and as if some bad news had just been known, we all make our silent way out of the place. But the spirits of the Peverils (of the living ones, that is to say) are the most mercurial imaginable, and the blight which the thought of handsome Dick and his doings casts over them passes away again with amazing rapidity.

A typical party, large, young, and peculiarly cheer-ful, was staying at Church-Peveril shortly after Christ-mas last year, and as usual on December 31, Mrs. Peveril was giving her annual New Year's Eve ball. The house was quite full, and she had commandeered as well the greater part of the Peveril Arms to provide sleeping-quarters for the overflow from the house. For some days past a black and windless frost had stopped all hunting, but it is an ill windlessness that blows no good (if so mixed a metaphor may be forgiven), and the lake below the house had for the last day or two been covered with an adequate and admirable sheet of ice. Everyone in the house had been occupied all the morning of that day in performing swift and violent ma-noeuvres on the elusive surface, and as soon as lunch was over we all, with one exception, hurried out again. This one exception was Madge Dalrymple who had had the misfortune to fall rather badly earlier in the day, but hoped, by resting her injured knee, instead of joining the skaters again, to be able to dance that evening. The hope, it is true, was of the most sanguine sort, for she could but hobble ignobly back to the house, but with the breezy optimism which characterises the Peverils (she is Blanche's first cousin), she remarked that it would be but tepid enjoyment that she could, in her present state, derive from further skating, and thus she sacrificed little, but might gain much.

Accordingly after a rapid cup of coffee which was served in the long gallery, we left Madge comfortably reclined on the big sofa at right-angles to the fireplace, with an attractive book to beguile the tedium till tea. Being of the family, she knew all about handsome Dick and the babies, and the fate of Mrs. Canning and Colonel Blantyre, but as we went out I heard Blanche say to her, "Don't run it too fine, dear," and Madge had replied, "No; I'll go away well before sunset." And so we left her alone in the long gallery.

Madge read her attractive book for some minutes, but failing to get absorbed in it, put it down and limped across to the window. Though it was still but little after two, it was but a dim and uncertain light that entered, for the crystalline brightness of the morning had given place to a veiled obscurity produced by flocks of thick clouds which were coming sluggishly up from the north-east. Already the whole sky was overcast with them, and occasionally a few snow flakes fluttered waveringly down past the long windows. From the darkness and bitter cold of the afternoon, it seemed to her that there was like to be a heavy snowfall before long, and these outward signs were echoed inwardly in her by that muffled drowsiness of the brain, which to those who are sensitive to the pressures and lightnesses of weather portends storm. Madge was peculiarly the prey of such external influences: to her a brisk morning gave an ineffable brightness and briskness of spirit, and correspondingly the approach of heavy weather produced a somnolence in sensation that both drowsed and depressed her.

It was in such mood as this that she limped back again to the sofa beside the log-fire. The whole house was comfortably heated by water-pipes, and though the fire of logs and peat, an adorable mixture, had been allowed to burn low, the room was very warm. Idly she watched the dwindling flames, not opening her book again, but lying on the sofa with face towards the fireplace, intending drowsily and not immediately to go to her own room and spend the hours, until the return of the skaters made gaiety in the house again, in writing one or two neglected letters. Still drowsily she began thinking over what she had to communicate: one letter several days overdue should go to her mother, who was immensely interested in the psychical affairs of the family. She would tell her how Master Anthony had been prodigiously active on the staircase a night or two ago, and how the Blue Lady, regardless of the severity of the weather, had been seen by Mrs. Peveril that morning, strolling about. It was rather interesting: the Blue Lady had gone down the laurel walk and had been seen by her to enter the stables, where, at the moment, Freddy Peveril was inspecting the frost-bound hunters. Identically then, a sudden panic had spread through the stables, and the horses had whinnied and kicked, and shied, and sweated. Of the fatal twins nothing had been seen for many years past, but, as her mother knew, the Peverils never used the long gallery after dark.

Then for a moment she sat up, remembering that she was in the long gallery now. But it was still but a little after half-past two, and if she went to her room in half an hour, she would have ample time to write this and another letter before tea. Till then she would read her book. But she found she had left it on the window-sill, and it seemed scarcely worth while to get it. She felt exceedingly drowsy.

The sofa where she lay had been lately re-covered, in a greyish green shade of velvet, somewhat the colour of lichen. It was of very thick soft texture, and she luxuriously stretched her arms out, one on each side of her body, and pressed her fingers into the nap. How horrible that story of Mrs. Canning was: the growth on her face was of the colour of lichen. And then without further transition or blurring of thought Madge fell asleep.

She dreamed. She dreamed that she awoke and found herself exactly where she had gone to sleep, and in exactly the same attitude. The flames from the logs had burned up again, and leaped on the walls, fitfully illuminating the picture of handsome Dick above the fire-place. In her dream she knew exactly what she had done to-day, and for what reason she was lying here now instead of being out with the rest of the skaters. She remembered also (still dreaming), that she was going to write a letter or two before tea, and prepared to get up in order to go to her room. As she half-rose she caught sight of her own arms lying out on each side of her on the grey velvet sofa. But she could not see where her hands ended, and where the grey velvet began: her fingers seemed to have melted into the stuff. She could see her wrists quite clearly, and a blue vein on the backs of her hands, and here and there a knuckle. Then, in her dream she remembered, the last thought which had been in her mind before she fell asleep, namely the growth of the lichen-coloured vegetation on the face and the eyes and the throat of Mrs. Canning. At that thought the strangling terror of real nightmare began: she knew that she was being transformed into this grey stuff, and she was absolutely unable to move. Soon the grey would spread up her arms, and over her feet; when they came in from skating they would find here nothing but a huge misshapen cushion of lichen-coloured velvet, and that would be she. The horror grew more acute, and then by a violent effort she shook herself free of the clutches of this very evil dream, and she awoke.

For a minute or two she lay there, conscious only of the tremendous relief at finding herself awake. She felt again with her fingers the pleasant touch of the velvet, and drew them backwards and forwards, assuring herself that she was not, as her dream had suggested, melting into greyness and softness. But she was still, in spite of the violence of her awakening, very sleepy, and lay there till, looking down, she was aware that she could not see her hands at all. It was very nearly dark.

At that moment a sudden flicker of flame came from the dying fire, and a flare of burning gas from the peat flooded the room. The portrait of handsome Dick looked evilly down on her, and her hands were visible again. And then a panic worse than the panic of her dreams seized her. Daylight had altogether faded, and she knew that she was alone in the dark in the terrible gallery. This panic was of the nature of nightmare, for she felt unable to move for terror. But it was worse than nightmare be cause she knew she was awake. And then the full cause of this frozen fear dawned on her; she knew with the certainty of absolute conviction that she was about to see the twin-babies.

She felt a sudden moisture break out on her face, and within her mouth her tongue and throat went suddenly dry, and she felt her tongue grate along the inner surface of her teeth. All power of movement had slipped from her limbs, leaving them dead and inert, and she stared with wide eyes into the blackness. The spurt of flame from the peat had burned itself out again, and darkness encompassed her.

Then on the wall opposite her, facing the windows, there grew a faint light of dusky crimson. For a moment she thought it but heralded the approach of the awful vision, then hope revived in her heart, and she remembered that thick clouds had overcast the sky before she went to sleep, and guessed that this light came from the sun not yet quite sunk and set. This sudden revival of hope gave her the necessary stimulus, and she sprang off the sofa where she lay. She looked out of the window and saw the dull glow on the horizon. But before she could take a step for ward it was obscured again. A tiny sparkle of light came from the hearth which did no more than illuminate the tiles of the fireplace, and snow falling heavily tapped at the window panes. There was neither light nor sound except these.

But the courage that had come to her, giving her the power of movement, had not quite deserted her, and she began feeling her way down the gallery. And then she found that she was lost. She stumbled against a chair, and, recovering herself, stumbled against another. Then a table barred her way, and, turning swiftly aside, she found herself up against the back of a sofa. Once more she turned and saw the dim gleam of the firelight on the side opposite to that on which she expected it. In her blind gropings she must have reversed her direction. But which way was she to go now? She seemed blocked in by furniture. And all the time insistent and imminent was the fact that the two innocent terrible ghosts were about to appear to her.

Then she began to pray, "Lighten our darkness, O Lord," she said to herself. But she could not remember how the prayer continued, and she had sore need of it. There was something about the perils of the night. All this time she felt about her with groping, fluttering hands. The fire-glimmer which should have been on her left was on her right again; therefore she must turn herself round again. "Lighten our darkness," she whispered, and then aloud she repeated, "Lighten our darkness."

She stumbled up against a screen, and could not remember the existence of any such screen. Hastily she felt beside it with blind hands, and touched something soft and velvety. Was it the sofa on which she had lain? If so, where was the head of it. It had a head and a back and feet—it was like a person, all covered with grey lichen. Then she lost her head completely. All that remained to her was to pray; she was lost, lost in this awful place, where no one came in the dark except the babies that cried. And she heard her voice rising from whisper to speech, and speech to scream. She shrieked out the holy words, she yelled them as if blaspheming as she groped among tables and chairs and the pleasant things of ordinary life which had become so terrible.

Then came a sudden and an awful answer to her screamed prayer. Once more a pocket of inflammable gas in the peat on the hearth was reached by the smouldering embers, and the room started into light. She saw the evil eyes of handsome Dick, she saw the little ghostly snow-flakes falling thickly outside. And she saw where she was, just opposite the door through which the terrible twins made their entrance. Then the flame went out again, and left her in blackness once more. But she had gained something, for she had her geography now. The centre of the room was bare of furniture, and one swift dart would take her to the door of the landing above the main staircase and into safety. In that gleam she had been able to see the handle of the door, bright-brassed, luminous like a star. She would go straight for it; it was but a matter of a few seconds now.

She took a long breath, partly of relief, partly to satisfy the demands of her galloping heart. But the breath was only half-taken when she was stricken once more into the immobility of nightmare.

There came a little whisper, it was no more than that, from the door opposite which she stood, and through which the twin-babies entered. It was not quite dark outside it, for she could see that the door was opening. And there stood in the opening two little white figures, side by side. They came towards her slowly, shufflingly. She could not see face or form at all distinctly, but the two little white figures were advancing. She knew them to be the ghosts of terror, innocent of the awful doom they were bound to bring, even as she was innocent. With the inconceivable rapidity of thought, she made up her mind what to do. She had not hurt them or laughed at them, and they, they were but babies when the wicked and bloody deed had sent them to their burning death. Surely the spirits of these children would not be inaccessible to the cry of one who was of the same blood as they, who had committed no fault that merited the doom they brought. If she entreated them they might have mercy, they might forebear to bring the curse on her, they might allow her to pass out of the place without blight, without the sentence of death, or the shadow of things worse than death upon her.

It was but for the space of a moment that she hesitated, then she sank down on to her knees, and stretched out her hands towards them.

"Oh, my dears," she said, "I only fell asleep. I have done no more wrong than that—"

She paused a moment, and her tender girl's heart thought no more of herself, but only of them, those little innocent spirits on whom so awful a doom was laid, that they should bring death where other children bring laughter, and doom for delight. But all those who had seen them before had dreaded and feared them, or had mocked at them.

Then, as the enlightenment of pity dawned on her, her fear fell from her like the wrinkled sheath that holds the sweet folded buds of Spring.

"Dears, I am so sorry for you," she said. "It is not your fault that you must bring me what you must bring, but I am not afraid any longer. I am only sorry for you. God bless you, you poor darlings."

She raised her head and looked at them. Though it was so dark, she could now see their faces, though all was dim and wavering, like the light of pale flames shaken by a draught. But the faces were not miserable or fierce—they smiled at her with shy little baby smiles. And as she looked they grew faint, fading slowly away like wreaths of vapour in frosty air.

* * *

Madge did not at once move when they had vanished, for instead of fear there was wrapped round her a wonderful sense of peace, so happy and serene that she would not willingly stir, and so perhaps disturb it. But before long she got up, and feeling her way, but without any sense of nightmare pressing her on, or frenzy of fear to spur her, she went out of the long gallery, to find Blanche just coming upstairs whistling and swinging her skates.

"How's the leg, dear," she asked, "You're not limping any more."

Till that moment Madge had not thought of it.

"I think it must be all right," she said, "I had forgotten it anyhow. Blanche, dear, you won't be frightened for me, will you, but—but I have seen the twins."

For a moment Blanche's face whitened with terror.

"What?" she said in a whisper.

"Yes, I saw them just now. But they were kind, they smiled at me, and I was so sorry for them. And somehow I am sure I have nothing to fear."

It seems that Madge was right, for nothing untoward has come to her. Something, her attitude to them, we must suppose, her pity, her sympathy, touched and dissolved and annihilated the curse. Indeed, I was at Church Peveril only last week, arriving there after dark. Just as I passed the gallery door, Blanche came out.

"Ah, there you are," she said, "I've just been seeing the twins. They looked too sweet and stopped nearly ten minutes. Let us have tea at once."

Winter Pastimes

This non-fiction article about winter tourism in Switzerland eventually developed into Benson's Winter Sports in Switzerland *(London: George Allen and Company, 1913). It is included here as background material, since the rest of the stories in this volume take place at Swiss skating resorts.*[34]

It is of invariable occurrence that when in our usually sub-tropical winters there is the smallest chance of the smallest piece of ice bearing, the whole adjacent population, regardless of other duties and even pleasures, flocks out to it with skates of some description, in order to enjoy this infrequent amusement. Annually, so we regret to see, a certain number of people are drowned in premature attempts to use skates; annually, also, an enormous number of enthusiastic folk are either totally or partially submerged in icy though insufficiently frozen water, because they cannot bear to lose a possible minute of tumbling about on the elusive surface. It is, therefore, reasonable to suppose that to the average mind there must be something peculiarly attractive about skating. If we heard that a particular field "bore," we should not all of us instantly go out to walk on it, with the possible chance of being suffocated in the earth below if we went through, and the excel-

---

34. First published as "Winter Pastimes," *The Windsor Magazine* 33, no. 192 (1911): 157–166.

lent chance of sinking in up to our knees in any case. No doubt the comparative rarity of this pursuit makes us more eager to enjoy these very occasional chances we get of indulging in it, but that alone would not be sufficient to account for the extraordinary rapidity with which the population makes for the frozen pond, or the extraordinary tardiness with which they leave it. In fact, there must be some inherent charm in skating—even though we put both feet down, and, in spite of that wise precaution, are the victims of the "frequent fall"—that makes us grab at any chance there may be of moving insecurely about on ice.

The reason is that the motion itself—that of sliding—is exquisite, even though the moments of gliding are punctuated by tumbles and collisions. We are accustomed to plod about at varying speeds on our feet, to roll about with carriage wheels or bicycle wheels below us; but who, except the dotard or the physically infirm, would dream of driving, or walking, or bicycling for purposes of pleasure if there was the chance of skating? For in skating, as, indeed, in the other winter sports to which it is akin, we enjoy a manner of locomotion which is the romance and the lyric of movement compared to the dull prose ground out by wheels or feet. Instead of stumping or rolling, we glide; friction—that acknowledged foe both to the pleasure of movement not less than of domestic life—is reduced to a minimum. That, too, is why we shall all fly so industriously in a year or two. Biplanes and monoplanes give movement without friction, except when they come to earth with undesigned rapidity, and give us our arrears of friction

Figure 7: The bobsleigh run at St. Moritz: A crew just starting.

in one lump sum; but in no other branches of motion than these ice-sports, except perhaps in swimming, do we get the same delicious quality of movement. And since swimming to a large extent partakes of this, that is why, whenever there is a brief spell of warm weather in our sub-Arctic summers, everyone who can swim betakes himself to the water.

Nothing shows more clearly how deep-rooted is this pleasure in the movement of gliding than the consideration of what we cheerfully risk, or of the inconvenience we undergo in order to gratify our taste. The possible penalty of a drowning, the probable one of a ducking, does not the least deter the average youth from venturing on insecure surfaces; while others of us go, at considerable expense, to covered-in rinks, and then make small edges on a totally insufficient and overcrowded area. Others—and these are the wisest and most determined of all—think nothing of a journey to Switzerland in mid-winter in order to be able to practise their sport there in the open air, with plenty of room to fall down in and plentiful manners of falling, with no risk of drowning, and a benignant and probably amused sun to look down on their efforts and warm them up to fresh exertions.

It is there in these high-Alp winter resorts, eyries between earth and heaven, that the three main winter pastimes, skating, tobogganing, and ski-ing (all gliding pursuits), can be enjoyed in perfection and under conditions which of themselves, without the addition of any of these pastimes at all, would be sufficient to make existence a day-long exhilaration. For the choking fogs

Figure 8: Bandy on the ice: Ladies v. men.

Figure 9: Skating at St. Moritz: On the Kulm Rink.

and dark dampness of the smoky town—should we be so unfortunate as to pass our blind winters in London—we take in exchange the turquoise skies of inimitable blue, and a great golden sun that marches across the azure field all day in unclouded triumph from the hour when he rises above the snow peaks in the steel-hued transparency of dawn till the time when he sets behind the flashed and crimson spears of the western Alps. Instead of lugubrious wading in the black mud and slush of London roadways, we walk forth to our pastime here with squeak and crunch of trodden snow; instead of having grimy puddles squirted at us by thunder-wheeled motor-'buses, the worst assault that can here be made on us is when a fairy puff of crystalline frost-flower is flicked at us by some upspringing tuft of pine which the sun has loosened from its binding. Occasionally, it is true, clouds gather, and a snow-storm may blot out the mountain for a couple of days, but we succeed without effort in forgetting all about that the moment the sun appears again. Once last year, in the middle of January, as this writer remembers, it rained. That was an outrage which it was not possible to allude to. There was probably some mistake; it did it by accident, not of malice.

Such are the conditions under which you have your fill of that divine winter pastime—the dry, frosty air—which everyone says is like champagne, though there is no kind of resemblance between the two—a sun that warms the inmost marrow of your bones, and the circle of pine wood crowned by great peaks to look on. And, if you choose to skate, there is no question as to whether

Figure 10: Skating at Davos.

the ice bears or whether you risk an immersion, for the rink is built up solid from the ground—a stretch of flawless ice obtained by continued floodings of a prepared and levelled place. Every night, too, when the skaters are gone home, and the rink has been carefully swept, the surface is flooded again or sprinkled with the hose, so that every morning a virgin sheet of ice lies waiting. And then, even if eternal youth was yours, and the glacial age descended again, so that you could skate from January to December, there would probably be some fresh intricacy of turn or edge to master; while, if you had three similarly endowed companions, it is certain that you would find some fresh weaving of figures in your combined sets.

The second of the three winter sports is tobogganing—a pursuit generally understood to have something to do with a tea-tray and a mound in the back-garden. But in Switzerland things are managed on a rather larger scale, and on your light iron sledge you whirl down miles of snow beaten hard by traffic. That is tobogganing in its simplest and most unsophisticated form: but, as in the case of the skating rink, art lends its aid, and at most of those Swiss winter resorts prepared roads are made either of beaten-down snow, or, in the swiftest and most exciting form, tracks banked up to take you round corners without running out are every evening sprinkled with water, so that the surface is hard, smooth ice. And when, on the Cresta run,[35] for instance, at St. Moritz, you see a padded figure face downwards on a skeleton or giant toboggan whirl

---

35. The Cresta run is still in use in 2020.

Figure 11: Driving a willing team.

Figure 12: Captain Dwyer, second in the Grand National Race, St. Moritz.

Figure 13: An uphill finish on the track at St. Moritz.

Figure 14: A nasty spill at Horseshoe Corner, on the bobsleigh run.

round the steep side of the banks at "Battledore" or "Shuttlecock," clinging like a fly to the steep wall of ice by sheer centrifugal force, or going down the last breathless descent at a speed that takes him high up the slope opposite, you will realise that there is a thrill and romance possible in mere motion which you have never hitherto suspected.

In both these branches of winter pastimes, constructive art has to prepare the playground of delight; in the third—ski-ing—you deal with snow-covered slopes in their natural state, and the more untouched they are, the better you are pleased. The skis themselves are strips of wood, from six to seven feet long and a few inches broad. They are fastened to the boots of the skier, who stands on them as on skates. Since they are smooth and polished on their under surface, and, owing to their length and the distribution of the skier's weight, do not sink deeply into the snow, it will be easily demonstrated by trial that if you put them on and stand on a steep hillside covered with crusted snow, the skis— and you on them—will instantly begin to slide down the hill with ever-increasing velocity. Then a variety of complicated things may happen: you may cross your ski-toes, and will at once fall violently sideways and forwards in the snow; your two feet may develop an inexplicable tendency to travel in different directions away from each other, and you will fall sideways or backwards; you may run into some hollow or inequality on your hillside, and will weave yourself and your skis into strange knots. Or—and this delightful result will occur more and more constantly as you persevere—you will

Figure 15: Top: Mr. Bott starting on his winning course in the Grand National Race on the Cresta Run. Bottom: Mr. Bott, winner of the Grand National Race three years in succession, on the Cresta Run.

Figure 16: Miss Wheble winning the Ladies' Grand National on the Cresta Run.

manage to stand fairly upright with your feet running in parallel lines, and you will hiss down your slope, with the snow spreading in feathers of frozen powder round your toes, like foam from the bows of a racing yacht, until you arrive at the bottom of your slope. Then, with ever-increasing facility, you will mount your slope again over snow into which you would sink up to your knees if you attempted to walk over it, passing lightly and easily over the surface, and do it all over again. By degrees you will learn the craft of your new art, tracing—with the help of the long pole you carry to steady yourself with—curving piths between obstacles, or practising turns, so that even in the midst of your swiftest descent you can turn completely round to right or left and face the upward slope again. And then, if you are very young, and strong, and brave, you will learn to jump on those long wooden boats, descending at full speed on your hillside to where a little artificial platform has been banked up in the snow. Over the edge of this you will fly into the empty air, touching ground again yards down on the continued slope.

Or, without being young or brave at all, you will set out in the morning with provender for the day, and, leaving the path, mount over fields of white untrodden snow till the pines are left below, and the shoulders of mountains that looked so high above you have melted into hummocks beneath your feet, and you ascend, you and your companions, and still ascend into the silence of the holy hills. Mixed with the climbing you will have swift ecstatic runs into collateral valleys, flashing from sunshine into the clear blue shadow of pine woods, and

Figure 17: Ski-ing on St. Moritz Lake.

Figure 18: Ski-ing at full speed.

Figure 19: Ski jumping competition at St. Moritz.

Figure 20: A curling match.

opposite you all the time the aiguilles of Charnounix and the great dome of Mont Blanc, clear-cut and crystalline, will climb with you. And there is more reward to come than even this thrill of penetrating into those white solitary places, for as the afternoon shadows begin to lengthen you will turn your face homeward again, and skim down over the snowfields with the hiss of frozen sprays, and in your heart the joy of the sun and the peace of the world and the ecstasy of motion and living.

It is not in any one of these multifarious factors in the great affairs of winter sports that the joy resides, for they all contribute to it. There is the sun, first of all, shining through perfectly dry, cold air. By some wonderful alchemy he takes the shiver out of the frost and leaves there the briskness. Then there is the perpetual snow—not snow as we understand it in England, a grey substance spotted with dirt which turns into muddy water when touched, but a fine dry powder that brushes off like dust, and leaves neither dirt nor damp behind. Then there are huge white mountains to look at, with black pine-woods on the lower slopes and a flawless blue sky bounding them above. All these things produce a feeling of vigour and health which predisposes to activity, and the methods of gratifying them are of the most delightful kind, for they are concerned with gliding at high speed. You may tumble and fall on your skates, you may be thrown head first out of your toboggan, or sideways from your skis into deep drifts of snow, but no thought of resentment at these accidents enters your head. For a minute or two, indeed, you

Figure 21: A ski-ing expedition.

may wonder if yon are hurt—or perhaps there may be no cause to wonder—yet all the time you know you do not care, and will before long be inviting another such injury by all the means in your power. And when the day is over, you are hungry for dinner and sleepy for bed, and in consequence probably sit up half the night dancing. Then in the morning you make haste to get breakfast over in order to do it all over again.

Yes, a joyful affair!

Figure 22: Awaiting their turn to go down the Cresta Run.

A Comedy of Styles

This story highlights the differences between the English and International styles of skating and pokes a bit of fun at English society at a Swiss resort in winter.[36]

The blaze of the January sun was pouring down on to the huge rink at Frédon, hot and invigorating, and yet by that inimitable conjuring trick which the sun so deftly performs all day in the high thin air of Alpine eyries, not melting one fragment of the ice, nor making the surface of it even soft. Above stretched steep pastures covered with fresh-fallen snow, and dotted with châlets fit to be hung on some immense Christmas tree, complete and toy-like with their little green-shuttered windows and their icicles depending from the snow-smothered eaves of the shingled roofs. Above, again, stretched the forest of pines, looking raven-black, where the snow had melted from off their tassels, against the shining dazzle of the white fields, while behind and beyond, remote and austere, rose the horns and precipices of the greater peaks.

Below, the ground declined sharply away: a few outlying châlets of the village stood in the foreground; beyond them the hillside leaped like a waterfall into the cloud-smothered valley of the Rhone, a couple of thousand feet below. Like a solid floor of grey mot-

---

36. First published as "A Comedy of Styles," *The Windsor Magazine* 39, no. 230 (February 1914): 331–335.

tled marble, this platform of cloud-land, as seen from above, stretched right across to the slopes on the far side of the valley, a floor level and motionless, fitted in with the cunning of some neat-jointed puzzle to the promontories and bays of the hills opposite. These, as they climbed upwards, rose again into the blaze of the midwinter sun, and guarding it all, like some great beast with head thrown back and paws outstretched, rose the shining snows of the Dent du Midi.

The rink, which had been crowded all morning, was emptying fast, for from the various hotels the bells had announced lunch-time, and there were but half a dozen enthusiasts left. Among those, enthusiastic to the point of mania, was Agnes Cartright, who, recuperating for a few minutes on a bench at the side of the ice, was utterly oblivious to the view and glory of the sun, and was entirely intent on a small and ragged pamphlet which she held in her hand, and which contained the list of the greedy requirements demanded of any who offered themselves as candidates for the first-class English test of skating. For the last three weeks she had lived, breathed, and dreamed skating; nothing else in the world seemed to her to matter at all, and if she had been awakened in the night by an armed inquisitor, who, with pistol to her head, had told her instantly to name the three greatest men in the world, she would have unhesitatingly have told him the names of three very fine skaters who were spending a month here. Two were to be her judges in the approaching test, the third was her brother, who, sitting beside her now with his mouth full of ham sandwich, was trying to explain to her the placing of one of those horrible and adored figures.

"Hold on to your back outside edge," he said, "till you get quite close to the centre, and change it at the centre. When you change it, don't wobble like a Channel boat in a cross-sea. Just change it. Hold on to your inside edge till you get half round the circle, then make your three, and—and stand still and go to sleep till you come back again to the centre. I don't see what bothers you in it."

"Skate it for me, Ted," she asked.

"Just when I'm lunching! You are the most selfish and inconsiderate—"

Figure 23: "'Just when I'm lunching! You are the most selfish and inconsiderate—'"

"I know. But I do want to see it done. It helps so enormously." He stood up, with half-eaten sandwich in one hand, a tall, satisfactory sort of young man, snub-nosed and sandy-haired, a sort of parody of the tip-tilted golden-haired girl who stood beside him. It was easy to see their relationship; the parody was unmistakable.

"I'll skate the whole set with you if you like," he said. "We've got the ice to ourselves."

"You *are* a darling. If I can get through this thing at all, it will be entirely your doing, Ted."

"Well, yes, mainly. All the same, you have got a certain natural aptitude."

Then followed a quarter of an hour of strenuous performance, as they wove the mystic dance, with its swift long edges and flicked turns, which is known as English combined skating. Whatever Agnes's power of execution might be, there was no question about the excellence of her style, as standing erect, yet not stiff, she swooped like a swallow into the centre, and sped out again to the circumference of the figure twenty yards away. It was impossible to see where the impetus for these bird-flights came from; they were as inexplicable as the movement of a soaring eagle, and her brother's speed was even more incomprehensible. He but seemed to lay his skate-blade on the ice and shot off with ever-increasing velocity. Their timing, too, from long-repeated practice together, was perfect; they passed each other at the centre with hardly a foot to spare between them, and soared away again. Occasionally he called a critical word to her, or made her repeat some evolution; but when, a quarter of an hour later, the practice was over, his praise was almost unfraternal.

"Yes, that will quite do," he said. "If you skate no worse than that, you will get through. Now, for Heaven's sake, let us finish lunch in peace."

She beamed appreciation of these high compliments.

"I'll just have ten minutes more alone," she said. "You might be an angel, Ted, and shout curses at me if I'm not up to the mark."

A young man, who had been watching this really charming performance, skated up to the bench where Ted was sitting, with arms and unemployed leg outstretched, in the approved and graceful International style. He really did rather resemble some flying Mercury, a pose which all skaters of his school do not attain with any marked degree of success. He had arrived here only the evening before, and nodded kindly to Ted, unaware of his immensity. In Agnes's opinion, this would be about equivalent to some criminal in the dock—skaters in the International style were all criminals in her eyes—negligently saluting the Lord Chief Justice on the bench.

"It really makes one doubt whether English skating is such a ramrod sort of performance as we think it," he said, "when you see a girl like that doing it. Isn't she at the Royal Hotel? I think I saw her there at the dance last night. You were skating with her, weren't you? What is her name?"

Ted Cartright looked at him with a rather pleasant

Figure 24: "'It really makes one doubt whether English skating is such a ramrod sort of performance.'"

mixture of amusement and resentment. The resentment was for this infernal patronage of the only real form of skating.

"Her name is Cartright," he said. "Miss Agnes Cartright. Perhaps I had better mention that my name is Cartright, too."

He paused a moment.

"In fact, I'm her brother," he said.

The flying Mercury laughed.

"Do you know, that's rather funny," he said. "Then, of course, you are *the* Mr. Cartright who skates. I assure you that the people I came up in the train with mentioned you with a sort of holy awe. And here am I telling you that perhaps English skating is not entirely a ramrod performance. But, really, I couldn't tell. I hope you don't mind. My name is Turner, if it's the slightest interest to you."

Ted Cartright laughed also.

"Then, of course, you are *the* Mr. Turner, if it comes to that," he said. "And your arrival has been spoken of with holy awe. You won all the cups and things last year, didn't you, in—in your style?"

"I suppose I did. It looks awful to you, doesn't it? A silly, showing-off, posing kind of game?"

"Well, I don't want to do it myself. I expect—"

Further attempts at compliments were interrupted by Agnes. "That was better, wasn't it, Ted?" she asked.

"I don't know; I wasn't looking. Agnes, may I introduce Mr. Turner to you?"

Mr. Turner, apparently, had already lunched, and soon left them. He skated off to the other side of the rink, and there took advantage of the empty ice. With flying, outstretched arms, he glided and poised and turned, launching himself at full speed on his hard, curved edges. He whirled in entrancing spirals, every inch and muscle of him was plastically part of woven loops and brackets. Anyone could see how masterly was his control, how vehement his force. Agnes turned to her brother. "It's really rather nice when it is done like that," she said. "You can see he is a—man."

"He doesn't in the least degree resemble a girl," said her brother. "Nor does he look like a cross between a hairdresser and a dancing-master, if that is what you mean."

"Yes, just that," she said. "But, of course, we can't call it skating. All the same—"

And she drank the remainder of Ted's beer.

Two days afterwards Agnes went up for her supreme trial. She was horribly nervous, and the sight of the reserved end of the rink, entirely emptied of skaters on her behalf, who lined the edges of it instead, made her think with bitter envy of Korah, Dathan, and Abiram,[37] those happy victims of the opening earth. But the moment she got under way, as soon as she felt her skate really bite the smooth, satin-like ice, she was conscious of nothing else but extreme exhilaration. Mr. Turner had left his International followers, who were standing about on one leg, in attitudes of extreme dejection, like hens on a wet day, and established himself on a seat in the sun, and the sight of him following her with perfectly undisguised admiration, made her

---

37. These biblical characters are described in Numbers 26:9-11.

not nervous, but immensely self-confident. Even the approving grunts of her brother, when in pauses she went and sat by him, did not lend her such solid encouragement. She had begged Mr. Turner not to come and watch her, when she danced—rather frequently—with him the night before at one of the hotel balls, and it may be added that she would have been extremely vexed if he had been so untrustworthy as to dream of keeping this promise she had extorted from him. In fact, as far as he was concerned, her state of mind is thus sufficiently indicated. Once or twice she made mistakes, which caused him much greater anxiety than they caused her. So his state of mind, as far as she was concerned, is also adequately outlined.

Ted skated excitedly up to her, after her judges had held but a brief conference.

"So that's floored," he said; "and now you can begin to learn to skate properly."

"Oh, Ted," she said, "do you mean I have passed?"

"Yes, of course. Let's have lunch."

Now, a certain proportion of the immigrant English at Frédon during the winter months think of practically nothing else all day, and a certain amount of the night, but ski-ing; to others, curling is a similar obsession; to others, tobogganing. But the greater number of the obsessed have no thoughts, day or night—except when they are actually engaged on some such frivolity as dancing, or dining, or bridge—but for skating. And the skaters, divided into two camps, as has been seen, the English style and the International, abstain, if polite, from passing the smallest criticism or taking the slightest notice of the other's doings; if impolite, they use such words as "ramrod" or "dancing-master." They have even been known to attempt to parody—with marked unsuccess—each other's styles. Consequently, rumours that began to creep about, some few days after Agnes Cartright had passed her first-class English test, thrilled these obsessed people to the core. Very early in the morning Miss Cartright had been seen on a sequestered corner of the rink with her unemployed leg wildly waving. With her arms she appeared to be swimming in short, ungainly strokes. An examination of the ice where these contortions had taken place showed beyond doubt that somebody had been trying to skate loops there—those dreadful, wicked, horrible loops which violated every rule of correct English style, to practise which laid the foundations for every immoral habit. It was true that, when observed, she made herself into a ramrod again and jerked her shoulders about in that distressing English manner, but later on, when the rink had cleared for lunch, she was seen again trying to do a spiral. Then she had been seen watching Mr. Turner for quite a long time that afternoon. This, of course, might be for other reasons, and the speaker—who had been doing just the same—wreathed her withered lips into what must have been a sarcastic smile. Such was the thrilling news brought into the International camp.

Later in the evening a spy came into the English camp. He had been on the rink that afternoon when dusk fell, and with his own eyes had seen a solitary figure in a withdrawn situation at the farther end, practising (apparently) in the English style. The speaker, at any rate, thought that these stiff, rigid attitudes, these jerked turns, were meant to be in distant emulation of it. With the amiable intention of assisting this ungainly struggler, and with a certain incredible conjecture in his mind, he skated up to him. The ungainly struggler, on seeing him approach, instantly began whirling his arms and legs again. It was Turner. And that night, after dinner, Turner had been seen again in the lounge of the hotel, absorbed in a book which was easily recognisable as one of the text-books of English skating.[38] Being observed, he hurriedly covered it up with a week-old copy of a daily paper, upside down, and pretended to be immersed in it. A little later he and Miss Cartright played bridge together, and it was credibly ascertained that neither of them had mentioned the word "skating" throughout the course of three long rubbers.

A week later all concealment was at an end. Agnes Cartright had openly joined the ranks of the Internationalists, while the star and mainstay of International skating was busy practising the English style, and hoped before the end of the season, if he was very industrious, to pass the third and most elementary of the English tests. What added to the comedy of the situation was that each went to the other for tuition, and each was at present hopelessly at sea. They, the pillars and ornaments of their schools, floundered and bungled, and were a source of the most blissful encourage-

---

38. Could the book Turner was reading be Benson's own book on skating, *English Figure Skating: A Guide to the Theory and Practice of Skating in the English Style*?

ment to other beginners. Occasionally a brief spell of apostasy would seize one or other of them, and Turner would giddily trace out a perfect back loop eight, or Miss Cartright, tall and swift and stable, would skim up to a centre from the distance of sixty yards, flick out a dream of a rocker, and hold the back edge for another sixty yards. But these were but infrequent weaknesses; for the most part, from morning till night, they were diligent with the alphabets of their respective studies. In the evening they often sat near each other, strenuously reading. Turner's book was a volume on the English style, with Agnes's name at the beginning; she read the text-book he had written himself.

A further thrill awaited Frédon, ten days later, when their engagement was made known. As for them, they had a great deal to say to each other on other subjects; but one sunny day, as they sat on the edge of the rink, in the lunch interval, the question which had really been a good deal in their minds found utterance. Agnes broached it.

"There's another thing we must talk about," she began.

"I know," he interrupted. "Skating, you mean. It's quite ridiculous to go on as we are. You see, I *had* to take to English skating when I saw you do it. I couldn't help myself. There was never anything so divine."

She laughed.

"Oh, Jack, that's just what happened to me. And here we are, dear, both making the most dreadful fools

of ourselves. I shall never be able to do it! I should be
utterly miserable about it if I wasn't so happy. What
is to be done?"

"We might toss up," he suggested. "The point is,
that we should both skate in the same style, isn't it?"

"Of course."

He took an Italian five-franc piece from his pocket.

"Heads, English style; tails, International," he suggested.

"Yes," said Agnes tremulously, and he spun the coin,
caught it, and opened his hand. And anyone who happens to be at Frédon this winter will see whether it was
heads or tails.

January

This excerpt from Benson's diary-like Book of Months *showcases a skater's winter vacation in Switzerland.*[39]

Thick yellow fog, and in consequence electric light to dress by and breakfast by, was the opening day of the year. Never, to anyone who looks at this fact in the right spirit, did a year dawn more characteristically. The denseness, the utter inscrutability of the face of that which should be, was never better typified. We blindly groped on the threshold of the future, feeling here for a bell-handle, here for a knocker, while the door still stood shut. Then, about mid-day, sudden commotions shook the vapours; dim silhouettes of house-roofs, promised lands perhaps, or profiled wrecks, stood suddenly out against swirling orange whirlpools of mist; and from my window, which commanded a double view up and down Oxford Street, I looked out over the crawling traffic, with an interest, as if in the unfolding of some dramatic plot, on the battle of the skies. From sick dead yellow the colour changed to gray, and for a few moments the street seemed lit by a dawn of April; then across the pearly tints came a sunbeam, lighting them with sudden opalescence. Then the smoke from the house opposite, which had been ascending slowly,

---

39. First published as "January" in *The Book of Months* (London: William Heinemann, 1903).

like a tired man climbing stairs, was plucked away by a breeze, and in two minutes the whole street was a blaze of primrose-coloured sunshine.

All that week I was work-bound in London—a place where, as everyone knows, there are forty-eight hours in every twenty-four. The reason for this is obvious. It is impossible to sit idly in a chair in London; it is impossible to read a book; and it is (happily) quite impossible to write one. Hence the hours are multiplied. The sound and spectacle of life induces a sort of intoxication of the mind. Ten yards of Piccadilly is a volume, and the Circus an improper epic. Hence the impossibility of reading; the books are in the flowing tides that jostle from house-wall to house wall, and they are vastly more entertaining than anything that publishers have ever had the good fortune to bring out.

Now, people who are incapable of reading book-print—of which the enormous mass is very sorry stuff—are held to be uneducated; but it seems to me that people who cannot read, or at any rate conjecture at, this splendid human print are much more ignorant. For it is here in these places, alive with the original words and phrases out of which all books are made, that there lies the key to all books that are worth reading at all. At any rate, here lies the material; it is here, and nowhere else, that the chef does his marketing. There are, however, several rules to be observed if you would read the original. The first is, that you must attend with all your might; the book, so to speak, shuts automatically if you cease to attend. The second is, that you must at a moment's notice be ready to pity and to praise. The third—and perhaps the most important of all—is, that you must never be shocked. For the whole attitude of the observer is covered by pity or praise. The Great Author does not want his moral condemnation, and, in addition to this, there is nothing so blinding to one's self as being shocked. It is like looking through a telescope at one point only, and that probably wrongly focussed; for it is focussed by one's own individual code, which is almost certainly wrong. It is Human Life you are looking at; if that is not good enough for you, go and look at something else. There are plenty of dull things in the world, but remember always that, if you find other people dull, it is only a sign that a dull person is present. But if you are to read the book Living, come humble and alert. Try to catch the point of every phrase, for of this you may be sure—that there is a point. You will find there, thank God! many pages that will make you laugh—laugh, that is, properly, with sheer childish, unreflecting amusement; you will find there things that will make you think; and you will certainly find there things that will make you want to weep. And if we knew a little, instead of knowing nothing, we should probably—no, certainly—fall on our knees, and thank God for that also.

One of each of these occurred to me to-day. The first was when I was coming out of the club with a friend on our way to dinner. An obsequious porter held the club door open, an obsequious page-boy stood by our glittering hansom, with a hand on the wheel. My friend had an opulent appearance and wore a fur coat. On the pavement were standing two exceedingly small and ragged boys, and one of them, whose hair dropped over his eyes like a Skye terrier, seeing this resplendent exit, put his thumbs in the place where the arm holes of his waistcoat would have been, had the merry little devil had one, and, with his nose in the air, said very loud to the other, "Whare are we doining to-night, Bill?"

The second made one laugh at first, but think afterwards, and it was thus: At the corner of Dover Street there lay a heap of mud and street sweepings, and as we drew up just opposite, blocked by an opposing tide of carriages in Piccadilly, a small, very dapper little gentleman in dress-clothes stepped into the middle of this muck-heap, with the result that one of his dress-pumps was drawn off his unfortunate foot with a "cloop" and stuck there. On to it there swooped a vulture of the highway, a lad of about twenty, who picked it out, and made off down Dover Street with it. Now, what good was one shoe to him? Would he not have done better to have wiped it carefully on his coat, which really could not have deteriorated farther, and chanced a tip from the dapper little gentleman? Or was the instinct of stealing so strong that he never stopped to think? One would have supposed that a tip was a practical certainty.

The third sight was merely a matter for tears.

I walked back from dinner, and my way lay up Piccadilly again. At a populous corner stood a very stout elderly woman, dressed in violent and ridiculous colours. Her hair was golden, her eyebrows broad, thick and vilely drawn, her cheeks so burned with rouge that one blushed. She addressed every passer by in endearing terms. None regarded her, That was quite right; but the pity of her standing there on this squally night, with her horrid mission and her total ill success! Yes, it is difficult to thank God for that.

After five days I got deliverance from the entrancing slavery, and, like a cork from a bottle, flew to Grindelwald.[40] The journey I remember as a dreadful dream, for I had a cold so bad that all sense of taste, smell, and most of hearing and feeling, had passed from me, and I seemed to myself to be a rough deal board being sent by train, and turned out into a drizzling night at what appeared to be mere cowsheds on the line, simply for the purpose of declaring that I had no spirit or lace about me. Spirit! The Queen of Sheba when she had seen Solomon in all his glory had more. As to lace, that diaphanous material seriously occupied my waking dreams as we mounted the Jura. Was there anything in my face that suggested lace, I wondered, or did lace frillings peep out from my trousers? Anyhow, why lace? I was really almost anxious to declare five hundred cigarettes, but nobody suggested such a thing. Then—

The new heaven and the new earth, an earth covered with powdery snow, thatched here and there by pines, and reaching beyond all power of thought, by glacier and snowfield and rocks too steep for the settling of the snow, into the pinnacles of the Eiger and the Wetterhorn. From ridge to ridge the eye followed, lost in amazement at the wonder of the earth and the greatness of its design. Austere and silent rose the virgin snows,

---

40. One of the skating resorts in Switzerland.

and more silent, growing from words to exclamation, and from exclamation to silence itself, one's wonder. There, out of the void and formless pulp which was once the world, they were set, barren, fruitless, useless, and that is the wonder of them and their glory. Centuries have been as but seconds in the life of an idle man in the forming of them; for centuries that have been to them but the winking of an eye they have raised their immemorial crests, and the centuries shall be as the sea-sand before they crumble. O ye Mountains and Hills, praise ye the Lord! Every day you praise Him.

Now, this "Book of Months" is almost certainly worth nothing, anyhow, and I take this opportunity to inform critics so, in case (as is not likely) they have the slighest doubt about it. But if they and I are wrong, it will be because we have both overlooked the possible value of a true document—true, that is, as far as I personally am able to make it true. Therefore I will state at once that for the next four weeks the childish pursuit of making correct lines and edges on the ice occupied me much more, except on a few occasions, than all the mountains, all the heavenly blue of the sky, or the divine radiance of the marching sun. Instead of attending to those big and beautiful things, I got up, day after day, full of anxious thoughts, and had I been assured that these anxieties would never trouble me again on condition that I never again looked at the Eiger, or the scarlet finger of the Finster-Aarhorn that caught the sunset long after the sun had set to us, I would quite certainly have closed with the bargain. Those who do not know what a clean outside-back counter means can have no voice in this affair, since they are not acquainted with the subject-matter of it, but those who do will, I believe, extend to me their pitying sympathy. For no known reason, I desired to make these and other turns, which when made are of no conceivable use to anybody, and full of anxious thoughts, which violent collisions with the elusive material on which I performed fully justified, I proceeded to devote the hours of light to these utterly indefensible pursuits. I wished to execute a movement in which the skate left a certain mark on the ice, and no other (I am alluding, of course, to involuntary change of edge), and to make these and other marks on the ice (continuous loops, bracket-eight, and a few more, for the sake of the curious) I signed a bond, so to speak, for three weeks of my short mortal life. All morning, that is to say, I struggled with these evanescent scratchings, ate a hurried lunch, and struggled again till it was dark. Really, it is very odd, and I hope to do the same next winter. I am perfectly aware that I could have spent my time much better, or, at any rate, tried to. I knew that at the time; but I did not care then, and I do not care now.

There were sane intervals, however. For instance, one Saturday evening it began to snow. Now, I see nothing conceivably wrong in skating on Sunday, and am unable to comprehend the position of those who do. But it is certainly wrong to skate on Sunday when it will spoil the ice on Monday, and on this particular Sunday I went to church in the morning, and afterwards took a sandwich lunch from the hotel, and, tying it securely to a toboggan, sat myself insecurely on the toboggan, and went alone—that was an essential part of the plan—down past the church and through the village, through fields of white snow that spouted as the toboggan met them, even as the spray spouts round the bows of a liner. In nothing, I suppose, does a man (unless he be M. Santos-Dumont[41]) come nearer to the ecstasy of flight, some low skimming flight that follows the contour of the ground as swallows when storm is imminent. So went I down an ever steepening mile, finishing at the end just by the side of the bridge that crosses the stream from the glacier. The frost had been severe for the last week, and this was nearly covered over with lids of ice that grew out from backwaters and extended almost from bank to bank. Wherever a stone stood in mid-current, there below it had the ice first gathered, groping its way downstream till the cold feeler reached another stone. Then, already half established, it had broadened and broadened till a third anchorage met it. But in certain swift places the water still ran unchecked, its flow, of course, greatly diminished with the lesser melting of the glacier in winter, but still busy, busy, seeking the sea with steadfast purpose. Round the banks and in the bed itself of the stream grew an immense company of alders covered completely with the inimitable confectionary of frost, a forest of spiked branches.

Then mounting again, I passed up a long gentle slope by a few outlying châlets, and, having come out of the shadow of the Eiger, sat down to lunch. The

---

41. Alberto Santos-Dumont (1873–1932) worked on developing flying machines.

air was utterly windless, the frost so keen that not a
flake of snow clung to my clothes, yet through the glory
of that pellucid air the sun struck so hot that a coat
was altogether a superfluity. Eastwards the Wetterhorn
rose in glacier and snowfield, and its superb and patient
beauty, as of some noble woman waiting for the man
she loves, struck me with a pang of delight. Thereafter, still climbing, I entered the pine-woods below the
Scheidegg, where the sun drew out a thousand wood-
land and resinous smells, as if odorous summer instead
of midwinter held sway.

Alone! I had intended to be alone, but never was
a man in more delectable company. Trees, glimpses of
the gorgeous dome above them, drifts of driven snow,
were my companions, while, if one grew overbold, there
was the Eiger to hazard a respectful remark to, and the
sun itself to be worshipped. On no other day, indeed,
that I can remember have I felt so strong a sympathy
with Parsees. High it swung, benignant, and all for the
fir-trees and me. Then rising higher, I came to the edge
of the wood and the beginning of the snowfields again,
and, resting for a moment, did an exceedingly childish
thing. Underneath a piece of spreading root of the last
tree of that heavenly wood I hid a Bryant and May's
match-box containing a stick of chocolate, an English
sixpence, two nickel coins of ten centimes, a short piece
of pencil, and four matches. These I dedicate to the
wayfarer should he need a light. Also I should ask him
to write his name with the pencil and put it in the
match-box, and, if he feels as foolish as I, add some
small object of no value. Next year I will go there

again, and make some further striking additions to the cache. The tree is a large one on the left of the path, and quite notably the last in the wood. My initials are rudely carved in the piece of root directly above the cache. An intelligent traveller knowing this can hardly miss the place.

Now, where shall we look for the origin of this instructive piece of foolishness? This is not a merely egotistic query, for I am perfectly certain that many sober and mature citizens like myself will feel sympathy with childishness that rejoices in such caches as I made on the slopes of the Scheidegg. Is it that we still preserve, even in this well-civilised and restauranted century, some cell in our brain which even now obeys the prudent instincts of some remote cave-dwelling ancestor, and do we now in play imitate his serious precautions? Or—and I like to think this better—have we still, in spite of our sober maturity, some remnants still of an heritage more priceless than cave-dwelling ancestors, namely, the lingering joys of our own childhood? On the whole, the evidence points this way, especially when I consider in connection with this certain other survivals, like that of "talking French." Here I feel that I may be treading on alien ground; the *cache* habit, I know, is not rare, but I have not at present met anyone who "talks French," of which the manner is as follows.

Everyone, I suppose, has moments of sheer physical enjoyment. I need mention two only: the one, getting into bed, with legs curled up, ere yet the freezing sheets can be encountered; the other, when very cold getting into a hot bath, a bath, that is to say, so hot that it is on the border between bliss and anguish, when, in fact, to move is to scream. On these occasions—for loneliness is essential,—I "talk French"; that is to say, streams of gibberish flow in a hushed voice from my lips, in the form of dialogue, and anyone present would hear remarkable things of this nature:

(With deep anxiety). "Usti Icibon?"

(Reassuringly) "Mimi molat isto pacher."

(Reassured) "Kaparando guilli. Amatinat skolot."

I blush to reproduce more. But I long to know if anybody else "talks French." I want to talk it with somebody, and compare vocabularies.

A long colloquy was held that afternoon, sitting in the sun, after the cache was made, and then towards sunset I started to go back through the pine-wood with dim but welcome thoughts of bears and brigands lying in wait on each side the path. One corner I remember I particularly feared, for low-growing bushes bordering the path might conceal almost anything. That I had good reason to fear it I soon found out, though I had feared it for wrong reasons, for my toboggan threw me with reckless gaiety into the middle of those same bushes. In fact, for the first half-mile the track was abominable; bare stones and tree-roots alternated with passages of breathless rapidity; never have I experienced a quicker succession of violences. But as the wood grew less dense the texture of the going became more uniform, and for the last mile I hissed downwards with ever-increasing speed and smoothness through the pallor of the snow-bright dusk. Large stars beamed luminous overhead, and from scattered cottages sprang the twinkling lights, showing that all were home from the frozen fields and safe within walls. Then, wonder of wonders the full moon rose over the top of the Wetterhorn with a light as clear as running water and as soft as sleep, making complete with its perfection this perfect day.

The other interlude from this rage of tracing useless marks on the ice was a funeral. The funeral was that of Slam's kitten, though the kitten was not really Slam's at all. But, to go back to the beginning of things, it is necessary that you should know who Slam was. Her real name was Evelyn Helen Anastasia, and goodness knows what; but what matters more is that she was a child six years and one month old, freckle-faced, snub-nosed, devoted to animals and the outside edge, and by far the most popular person in the hotel. It was the outside edge originally that had brought us together, for she had told me that I didn't do it properly, and, very kindly showing me how, she had fallen heavily on the ice. As I picked her up, she said:

"You see what I mean, don't you? Let me show you again."

Under her tuition I improved, and, what was more important, our friendship ripened. I am proud to think that I was the only person who ever heard about the kitten, which had followed Slam—I am sure I don't wonder—with pitiful mewings, down from the Happy Valley, an ownerless beast that would have touched hearts more hard than Slam's. She kept it in a cupboard in her room and fed it with cake. This I learned on the second day of the kitten's imprisonment. That evening it died. I will pass over Slam's lamentations, and the wealth of falsehood by which I convinced her that a diet of cake in an airless cupboard was the only thing that could have saved it. Then, as it was dead, it had to be buried, still without the cognizance of Slam's nurse, whom I feared.

"I don't want a lot of people," said Slam. "It would be much nicer if we buried her quietly. So when nurse is at dinner I will bring her down in my hat."

Meantime I had procured a cardboard box, and from Slam's hat the kitten passed into its coffin. The coffin was put on our toboggan—for Slam and I were going to lunch out—and the catafalque left the hotel.

Slam put her hand into mine—a compliment that only children can pay—and we debated about the cemetery. I personally inclined to the river-bed at the bottom of the valley, but Slam would have none of it.

"Up above," she said, "it is cleaner;" and, though it was all pretty clean, I assented. "Then we can eat our lunch and toboggan down," she added. This was common-sense; to walk up after the funeral would be depressing; we might recover our lightness of spirit if we left the tobogganing till afterwards.

On the way up, through the village, that is, and towards the glacier, the talk turned on serious subjects. Did I believe that animals would have a resurrection? Why did God make them if they were just to die and be finished? Again, if they were to have a resurrection, was it not proper to bury them properly? Thus we arrived at the cemetery. Four pine-trees stood there, with snow drifted high between them; the benediction of the sun hallowed the place; never had anyone a more virgin tomb. We scooped out the snow down to soil-level, and dropped the box into the excavation. Then with pious hands we covered it up, and on the top of the cairn planted sprigs taken from the pines.

"And now I will say my prayers," said Slam.

She knelt down in the snow, and, even with the fear of her nurse before my eyes, I could say nothing to dissuade her, but knelt by her and uncovered my head. And then Slam said the Lord's Prayer, and asked that she might be a good girl always, and prayed that God might bless her father and mother and nurse and me.

Do you know what it is to be remembered in the prayers of a child? Then she paused: "and the kitten," she added. And I said "Amen."

So there the kitten lies, between the sky and the beautiful snow-clad earth. Pines whisper about it, and the Wetterhorn and Eiger watch over its resting-place. And Slam said her prayers there.

What follows? As far as I am concerned, this: I believe that the whole creation groaneth and travaileth in pain together, and that there will be one day a great healing and comforting. And when on that day, mysteriously, unintelligibly, that little body, which meantime has fed the grasses and the alpine flowers of the place, comes to itself and is alive again, I believe that a happy little kitten will stand between those four pine-trees, lost no longer. And Slam and I will recognize it. And the kitten—who knows?—will recognize us, and Slam will say again, in the phrase that is so often on her lips:

"Oh, it is nice!"

The Other Bed

Not all trips to Switzerland were filled with outdoor fun. When the weather prohibits skating, this story's English visitor to Switzerland has a terrifying experience.[42]

I had gone out to Switzerland just before Christmas, expecting, from experience, a month of divinely renovating weather, of skating all day in brilliant sun, and basking in the hot frost of that windless atmosphere. Occasionally, as I knew, there might be a snowfall, which would last perhaps for forty-eight hours at the outside, and would be succeeded by another ten days of cloudless perfection, cold even to zero at night, but irradiated all day long by the unflecked splendour of the sun.

Instead the climatic conditions were horrible. Day after day a gale screamed through this upland valley that should have been so windless and serene, bringing with it a tornado of sleet that changed to snow by night. For ten days there was no abatement of it, and evening after evening, as I consulted my barometer, feeling sure that the black finger would show that we were coming to the end of these abominations, I found that it had sunk a little lower yet, till it stayed, like a homing pigeon, on the S of storm. I mention these things in depreciation of the story that follows, in order that the intelligent reader may say at once, if he wishes, that all that oc-

---

42. From *The Room in the Tower and Other Stories.*

curred was merely a result of the malaise of nerves and digestion that perhaps arose from those storm-bound and disturbing conditions. And now to go back to the beginning again.

I had written to engage a room at the Hôtel Beau Site, and had been agreeably surprised on arrival to find that for the modest sum of twelve francs a day I was allotted a room on the first floor with two beds in it. Otherwise the hotel was quite full. Fearing to be billeted in a twenty-two-franc room by mistake, I instantly confirmed my arrangements at the bureau. There was no mistake: I had ordered a twelve-franc room and had been given one. The very civil clerk hoped that I was satisfied with it, for otherwise there was nothing vacant. I hastened to say that I was more than satisfied, fearing the fate of Esau.[43]

I arrived about three in the afternoon of a cloudless and glorious day, the last of the series. I hurried down to the rink, having had the prudence to put skates in the forefront of my luggage, and spent a divine but struggling hour or two, coming up to the hotel about sunset. I had letters to write, and after ordering tea to be sent up to my gorgeous apartment, No. 23, on the first floor, I went straight up there.

The door was ajar and—I feel certain I should not even remember this now except in the light of what followed—just as I got close to it, I heard some faint movement inside the room and instinctively knew that my servant was there unpacking. Next moment I was in the room myself, and it was empty. The unpacking

---

43. Esau gave up his birthright in Genesis 25.

had been finished, and everything was neat, orderly, and comfortable. My barometer was on the table, and I observed with dismay that it had gone down nearly half an inch. I did not give another thought to the movement I thought I had heard from outside.

Certainly I had a delightful room for my twelve francs a day. There were, as I have said, two beds in it, on one of which were already laid out my dress-clothes, while night-things were disposed on the other. There were two windows, between which stood a large washing-stand, with plenty of room on it; a sofa with its back to the light stood conveniently near the pipes of central heating, there were a couple of good arm-chairs, a writing table, and, rarest of luxuries, another table, so that every time one had breakfast it was not necessary to pile up a drift of books and papers to make room for the tray. My window looked east, and sunset still flamed on the western faces of the virgin snows, while above, in spite of the dejected barometer, the sky was bare of clouds, and a thin slip of pale crescent moon was swung high among the stars that still burned dimly in these first moments of their kindling. Tea came up for me without delay, and, as I ate, I regarded my surroundings with extreme complacency.

Then, quite suddenly and without cause, I saw that the disposition of the beds would never do; I could not possibly sleep in the bed that my servant had chosen for me, and without pause I jumped up, transferred my dress clothes to the other bed, and put my night things where they had been. It was done breathlessly almost, and not till then did I ask myself why I had done it.

I found I had not the slightest idea. I had merely felt that I could not sleep in the other bed. But having made the change I felt perfectly content.

My letters took me an hour or so to finish, and I had yawned and blinked considerably over the last one or two, in part from their inherent dullness, in part from quite natural sleepiness. For I had been in the train for twenty-four hours, and was fresh to these bracing airs which so conduce to appetite, activity, and sleep, and as there was still an hour before I need dress, I lay down on my sofa with a book for excuse, but the intention to slumber as reason. And consciousness ceased as if a tap had been turned off.

Then—I dreamed. I dreamed that my servant came very quietly into the room, to tell me no doubt that it was time to dress. I supposed there were a few minutes to spare yet, and that he saw I was dozing, for, instead of rousing me, he moved quietly about the room, setting things in order. The light appeared to me to be very dim, for I could not see him with any distinctness, indeed, I only knew it was he because it could not be anybody else. Then he paused by my washing-stand, which had a shelf for brushes and razors above it, and I saw him take a razor from its case and begin stropping it; the light was strongly reflected on the blade of the razor. He tried the edge once or twice on his thumb nail, and then to my horror I saw him trying it on his throat. Instantaneously one of those deafening dream-crashes awoke me, and I saw the door half open, and my servant in the very act of coming in. No doubt the opening of the door had constituted the crash.

I had joined a previously-arrived party of five, all of us old friends, and accustomed to see each other often, and at dinner, and afterwards in intervals of bridge, the conversation roamed agreeably over a variety of topics, rocking-turns and the prospects of weather (a thing of vast importance in Switzerland, and not a commonplace subject) and the performances at the opera, and under what circumstances as revealed in dummy's hand, is it justifiable for a player to refuse to return his partner's original lead in no trumps. Then over whisky and soda and the repeated "last cigarette," it veered back via the Zantzigs to thought transference and the transference of emotion. Here one of the party, Harry Lambert, put forward the much discussed explanation of haunted houses based on this principle. He put it very concisely.

"Everything that happens," he said, "whether it is a step we take, or a thought that crosses our mind, makes some change in its immediate material world. Now the most violent and concentrated emotion we can imagine is the emotion that leads a man to take so extreme a step as killing himself or somebody else. I can easily imagine such a deed so eating into the material scene, the room or the haunted heath, where it happens, that its mark lasts an enormous time. The air rings with the cry of the slain and still drips with his blood. It is not everybody who will perceive it, but sensitives will. By the way, I am sure that man who waits on us at dinner is a sensitive."

It was already late, and I rose.

"Let us hurry him to the scene of a crime," I said.
"For myself I shall hurry to the scene of sleep."

* * *

Outside the threatening promise of the barometer
was already finding fulfilment, and a cold ugly wind
was complaining among the pines, and hooting round
the peaks, and snow had begun to fall. The night was
thickly overcast, and it seemed as if uneasy presences
were going to and fro in the darkness. But there was
no use in ill augury, and certainly if we were to be
house-bound for a few days I was lucky in having so
commodious a lodging. I had plenty to occupy myself
with indoors, though I should vastly have preferred to
be engaged outside, and in the immediate present how
good it was to lie free in a proper bed after a cramped
night in the train.

* * *

I was half-undressed when there came a tap at my
door, and the waiter who had served us at dinner came
in carrying a bottle of whisky. He was a tall young
fellow, and though I had not noticed him at dinner, I
saw at once now, as he stood in the glare of the electric
light, what Harry had meant when he said he was sure
he was a sensitive. There is no mistaking that look: it
is exhibited in a peculiar "inlooking" of the eye. Those
eyes, one knows, see further than the surface...

"The bottle of whisky for monsieur," he said, putting
it down on the table.

"But I ordered no whisky," said I.

He looked puzzled.

"Number twenty-three?" he said.

Then he glanced at the other bed.

"Ah, for the other gentleman, without doubt," he said.

"But there is no other gentleman," said I. "I am alone here."

He took up the bottle again.

"Pardon, monsieur," he said. "There must be a mistake. I am new here; I only came to-day. But I thought—"

"Yes?" said I. "I thought that number twenty-three had ordered a bottle of whisky," he repeated. "Good-night, monsieur, and pardon."

* * *

I got into bed, extinguished the light, and feeling very sleepy and heavy with the oppression, no doubt, of the snow that was coming, expected to fall asleep at once. Instead my mind would not quite go to roost, but kept sleepily stumbling about among the little events of the day, as some tired pedestrian in the dark stumbles over stones instead of lifting his feet. And as I got sleepier it seemed to me that my mind kept moving in a tiny little circle. At one moment it drowsily recollected how I had thought I had heard movement inside my room, at the next it remembered my dream of some figure going stealthily about and stropping a razor, at a third it wondered why this Swiss waiter with the eyes of a "sensitive" thought that number twenty-three had ordered a bottle of whisky. But at the time I made no guess as to any coherence between these little isolated facts; I only dwelt on them with drowsy persistence. Then a fourth fact came to join the sleepy circle, and I wondered why I had felt a repugnance against using the other bed. But there was no explanation of this forthcoming, either, and the outlines of thought grew more blurred and hazy, until I lost consciousness altogether.

* * *

Next morning began the series of awful days, sleet and snow falling relentlessly with gusts of chilly wind, making any out-of-door amusement next to impossible. The snow was too soft for toboganning, it balled on the skis, and as for the rink it was but a series of pools of slushy snow. This in itself, of course, was quite enough to account for any ordinary depression and heaviness of spirit, but all the time I felt there was something more than that to which I owed the utter blackness that hung over those days. I was beset too by fear that at first was only vague, but which gradually became more definite, until it resolved itself into a fear of number twenty-three and in particular a terror of the other bed. I had no notion why or how I was afraid of it, the thing was perfectly causeless, but the shape and the outline of it grew slowly clearer, as detail after detail of ordinary life, each minute and trivial in itself, carved and moulded this fear, till it became definite. Yet the whole thing was so causeless and childish that I could speak to no one of it; I could but assure myself that it was all a figment of nerves disordered by this unseemly weather.

However, as to the details, there were plenty of them. Once I woke up from strangling nightmare, unable at first to move, but in a panic of terror, believing that I was sleeping in the other bed. More than once, too, awaking before I was called, and getting out of bed to look at the aspect of the morning, I saw with a sense of dreadful misgiving that the bed-clothes on the other bed were strangely disarranged, as if some one had slept there, and smoothed them down afterwards, but not so well as not to give notice of the occupation. So one night I laid a trap, so to speak, for the intruder, of which the real object was to calm my own nervousness (for I still told myself that I was frightened of nothing), and tucked in the sheet very carefully, laying the pillow on the top of it. But in the morning it seemed as if my interference had not been to the taste of the occupant, for there was more impatient disorder than usual in the bed-clothes, and on the pillow was an indentation, round and rather deep, such as we may see any morning in our own beds. Yet by day these things did not frighten me, but it was when I went to bed at night that I quaked at the thought of further developments.

It happened also from time to time that I wanted something brought me, or wanted my servant. On three or four of these occasions my bell was answered by the "Sensitive," as we called him, but the Sensitive, I noticed, never came into the room. He would open the door a chink to receive my order, and on returning would again open it a chink to say that my boots, or whatever it was, were at the door. Once I made him come in, but I saw him cross himself as, with a face of icy terror, he stepped into the room, and the sight somehow did not reassure me. Twice also he came up in the evening, when I had not rung at all, even as he came up the first night, and opened the door a chink to say that my bottle of whisky was outside. But the poor fellow was in a state of such bewilderment when I went out and told him that I had not ordered whisky, that I did not press for an explanation. He begged my pardon profusely; he thought a bottle of whisky had been ordered for number twenty-three. It was his mistake, entirely—I should not be charged for it; it must have been the other gentleman. Pardon again; he remembered there was no other gentleman, the other bed was unoccupied.

It was on the night when this happened for the second time that I definitely began to wish that I too was quite certain that the other bed was unoccupied. The ten days of snow and sleet were at an end, and to-night the moon once more, grown from a mere slip to a shining shield, swung serenely among the stars. But though at dinner everyone exhibited an extraordinary change of spirit, with the rising of the barometer and the discharge of this huge snow-fall, the intolerable gloom which had been mine so long but deepened and blackened. The fear was to me now like some statue, nearly finished, modelled by the carving hands of these details, and though it still stood below its moistened sheet, any moment, I felt, the sheet might be twitched away, and I be confronted with it. Twice that evening I had started to go to the bureau, to ask to have a bed made up for me, anywhere, in the billiard-room or the smoking-room, since the hotel was full, but the intolerable childishness of the proceeding revolted me. What was I afraid of? A dream of my own, a mere nightmare? Some fortuitous disarrangement of bed-linen? The fact that a Swiss waiter made mistakes about bottles of whisky? It was an impossible cowardice.

But equally impossible that night were billiards or bridge, or any form of diversion. My only salvation seemed to lie in downright hard work, and soon after dinner I went to my room (in order to make my first real counter-move against fear) and sat down solidly to several hours of proof-correcting, a menial and monotonous employment, but one which is necessary, and engages the entire attention. But first I looked thoroughly round the room, to reassure myself, and found all modern and solid; a bright paper of daisies on the wall, a floor parquetted, the hot-water pipes chuckling to themselves in the corner, my bed-clothes turned down for the night, the other bed—

The electric light was burning brightly, and there seemed to me to be a curious stain, as of a shadow, on the lower part of the pillow and the top of the sheet, definite and suggestive, and for a moment I stood there again throttled by a nameless terror. Then taking my courage in my hands I went closer and looked at it. Then I touched it; the sheet, where the stain or shadow was, seemed damp to the hand, so also was the pillow. And then I remembered; I had thrown some wet clothes on the bed before dinner. No doubt that was the reason. And fortified by this extremely simple dissipation of my fear, I sat down and began on my proofs. But my fear had been this, that the stain had not in that first moment looked like the mere greyness of water-moistened linen.

From below, at first, came the sound of music, for they were dancing to-night, but I grew absorbed in my work, and only recorded the fact that after a time there was no more music. Steps went along the passages, and I heard the buzz of conversation on landings, and the closing of doors till by degrees the silence became noticeable. The loneliness of night had come.

It was after the silence had become lonely that I made the first pause in my work, and by the watch on my table saw that it was already past midnight. But I had little more to do; another half-hour would see the end of the business, but there were certain notes I had to make for future reference, and my stock of paper was already exhausted. However, I had bought some in the village that afternoon, and it was in the bureau downstairs, where I had left it, when I came in and had subsequently forgotten to bring it upstairs. It would be the work of a minute only to get it.

The electric light had brightened considerably during the last hour, owing no doubt to many burners being put out in the hotel, and as I left the room I saw again the stain on the pillow and sheet of the other bed. I had really forgotten all about it for the last hour, and its presence there came as an unwelcome surprise. Then I remembered the explanation of it, which had struck me before, and for purposes of self-reassurement I again touched it. It was still damp, but—Had I got chilly with my work? For it was warm to the hand. Warm, and surely rather sticky. It did not seem like the touch of the water-damp. And at the same moment I knew I was not alone in the room. There was something there, something silent as yet, and as yet invisible. But it was there.

Now for the consolation of persons who are inclined to be fearful, I may say at once that I am in no way brave, but that terror which, God knows, was real e- nough, was yet so interesting, that interest over ruled it. I stood for a moment by the other bed, and, half-con- sciously only, wiped the hand that had felt the stain, for the touch of it, though all the time I told myself that it was but the touch of the melted snow on the coat I had put there, was unpleasant and unclean. More than that I did not feel, because in the presence of the unknown and the perhaps awful, the sense of curiosity, one of the strongest in stincts we have, came to the fore. So, rather eager to get back to my room again, I ran downstairs to get the packet of paper. There was still a light in the bureau, and the Sensitive, on night-duty, I suppose, was sitting there dozing. My entrance did not disturb him, for I had on noiseless felt slippers, and seeing at once the package I was in search of, I took it, and left him still unawakened. That was somehow of a fortifying nature. The Sensitive anyhow could sleep in his hard chair; the occupant of the unoccupied bed was not calling to him to-night.

I closed my door quietly, as one does at night when the house is silent, and sat down at once to open my packet of paper and finish my work. It was wrapped up in an old news-sheet, and struggling with the last of the string that bound it, certain words caught my eye. Also the date at the top of the paper caught my eye, a date nearly a year old, or, to be quite accurate, a date fifty-one weeks old. It was an American paper and what it recorded was this:

"The body of Mr. Silas R. Hume, who committed suicide last week at the Hôtel Beau Site, Moulin sur Chalons, is to be buried at his house in Boston, Mass. The inquest held in Switzerland showed that he cut his throat with a razor, in an attack of delirium tremens induced by drink. In the cupboard of his room were found three dozen empty bottles of Scotch whisky..."

So far I had read when without warning the electric light went out, and I was left in, what seemed for the moment, absolute darkness. And again I knew I was not alone, and I knew now who it was who was with me in the room.

Then the absolute paralysis of fear seized me. As if a wind had blown over my head, I felt the hair of it stir and rise a little. My eyes also, I suppose, became accustomed to the sudden darkness, for they could now perceive the shape of the furniture in the room from the light of the starlit sky outside. They saw more too than the mere furniture. There was standing by the wash-stand between the two windows a figure, clothed only in night-garments, and its hands moved among the objects on the shelf above the basin. Then with two steps it made a sort of dive for the other bed, which was in shadow. And then the sweat poured on to my forehead.

Though the other bed stood in shadow I could still see dimly, but sufficiently, what was there. The shape of a head lay on the pillow, the shape of an arm lifted its hand to the electric bell that was close by on the wall, and I fancied I could hear it distantly ringing. Then a moment later came hurrying feet up the stairs and along the passage outside, and a quick rapping at my door.

"Monsieur's whisky, monsieur's whisky," said a voice just outside. "Pardon, monsieur, I brought it as quickly as I could."

The impotent paralysis of cold terror was still on me. Once I tried to speak and failed, and still the gentle tapping went on at the door, and the voice telling some one that his whisky was there. Then at a second attempt, I heard a voice which was mine saying hoarsely:

"For God's sake come in; I am alone with it."

* * *

There was the click of a turned door-handle, and as suddenly as it had gone out a few seconds before, the electric light came back again, and the room was in full illumination. I saw a face peer round the corner of the door, but it was at another face I looked, the face of a man sallow and shrunken, who lay in the other bed, staring at me with glazed eyes. He lay high in bed, and his throat was cut from ear to ear; and the lower part of the pillow was soaked in blood, and the sheet streamed with it.

* * *

Then suddenly that hideous vision vanished, and there was only a sleepy-eyed waiter looking into the room. But below the sleepiness terror was awake, and his voice shook when he spoke.

"Monsieur rang?" he asked.

No, monsieur had not rung. But monsieur made himself a couch in the billiard-room.

The Horror-Horn

Although skating takes a back seat in this Alpine tale of terror, skates play an important role.[44]

For the past ten days Alhubel had basked in the radiant midwinter weather proper to its eminence of over 6,000 feet. From rising to setting the sun (so surprising to those who have hitherto associated it with a pale, tepid plate indistinctly shining through the murky air of England) had blazed its way across the sparkling blue, and every night the serene and windless frost had made the stars sparkle like illuminated diamond dust. Sufficient snow had fallen before Christmas to content the skiers, and the big rink, sprinkled every evening, had given the skaters each morning a fresh surface on which to perform their slippery antics. Bridge and dancing served to while away the greater part of the night, and to me, now for the first time tasting the joys of a winter in the Engadine, it seemed that a new heaven and a new earth had been lighted, warmed, and refrigerated for the special benefit of those who like myself had been wise enough to save up their days of holiday for the winter.

But a break came in these ideal conditions: one afternoon the sun grew vapour-veiled and up the valley from the north-west a wind frozen with miles of travel

---

44. From *Visible and Invisible* (London: Hutchinson and Co., 1923).

over ice-bound hill-sides began scouting through the calm halls of the heavens. Soon it grew dusted with snow, first in small flakes driven almost horizontally before its congealing breath and then in larger tufts as of swansdown. And though all day for a fortnight before the fate of nations and life and death had seemed to me of far less importance than to get certain tracings of the skate-blades on the ice of proper shape and size, it now seemed that the one paramount consideration was to hurry back to the hotel for shelter: it was wiser to leave rocking-turns[45] alone than to be frozen in their quest.

I had come out here with my cousin, Professor Ingram, the celebrated physiologist and Alpine climber. During the serenity of the last fortnight he had made a couple of notable winter ascents, but this morning his weather-wisdom had mistrusted the signs of the heavens, and instead of attempting the ascent of the Piz Passug he had waited to see whether his misgivings justified themselves. So there he sat now in the hall of the admirable hotel with his feet on the hot-water pipes and the latest delivery of the English post in his hands. This contained a pamphlet concerning the result of the Mount Everest expedition, of which he had just finished the perusal when I entered.

"A very interesting report," he said, passing it to me, "and they certainly deserve to succeed next year. But who can tell, what that final six thousand feet may entail? Six thousand feet more when you have already accomplished twenty-three thousand does not seem much,

---

45. Rockers in today's skating parlance.

but at present no one knows whether the human frame can stand exertion at such a height. It may affect not the lungs and heart only, but possibly the brain. Delirious hallucinations may occur. In fact, if I did not know better, I should have said that one such hallucination had occurred to the climbers already."

"And what was that?" I asked.

"You will find that they thought they came across the tracks of some naked human foot at a great altitude. That looks at first sight like an hallucination. What more natural than that a brain excited and exhilarated by the extreme height should have interpreted certain marks in the snow as the footprints of a human being? Every bodily organ at these altitudes is exerting itself to the utmost to do its work, and the brain seizes on those marks in the snow and says 'Yes, I'm all right, I'm doing my job, and I perceive marks in the snow which I affirm are human footprints.' You know, even at this altitude, how restless and eager the brain is, how vividly, as you told me, you dream at night. Multiply that stimulus and that consequent eagerness and restlessness by three, and how natural that the brain should harbour illusions! What after all is the delirium which often accompanies high fever but the effort of the brain to do its work under the pressure of feverish conditions? It is so eager to continue perceiving that it perceives things which have no existence!"

"And yet you don't think that these naked human footprints were illusions," said I. "You told me you would have thought so, if you had not known better."

He shifted in his chair and looked out of the window

a moment. The air was thick now with the density of the big snow-flakes that were driven along by the squealing north-west gale.

"Quite so," he said. "In all probability the human footprints were real human footprints. I expect that they were the footprints, anyhow, of a being more nearly a man than anything else. My reason for saying so is that I know such beings exist. I have even seen quite near at hand—and I assure you I did not wish to be nearer in spite of my intense curiosity—the creature, shall we say, which would make such footprints. And if the snow was not so dense, I could show you the place where I saw him."

He pointed straight out of the window, where across the valley lies the huge tower of the Ungeheuerhorn[46] with the carved pinnacle of rock at the top like some gigantic rhinoceros-horn. On one side only, as I knew, was the mountain practicable, and that for none but the finest climbers; on the other three a succession of ledges and precipices rendered it unscalable. Two thousand feet of sheer rock form the tower; below are five hundred feet of fallen boulders, up to the edge of which grow dense woods of larch and pine.

"Upon the Ungeheuerhorn?" I asked.

"Yes. Up till twenty years ago it had never been ascended, and I, like several others, spent a lot of time in trying to find a route up it. My guide and I sometimes spent three nights together at the hut beside the

---

46. The German word "ungeheuer" can mean both enormous and monstrous. "Horror-Horn" is a rough translation of "Ungeheuerhorn."

Blumen glacier, prowling round it, and it was by luck really that we found the route, for the mountain looks even more impracticable from the far side than it does from this. But one day we found a long, transverse fissure in the side which led to a negotiable ledge; then there came a slanting ice couloir which you could not see till you got to the foot of it. However, I need not go into that."

The big room where we sat was filling up with cheerful groups driven indoors by this sudden gale and snowfall, and the cackle of merry tongues grew loud. The band, too, that invariable appanage of tea-time at Swiss resorts, had begun to tune up for the usual potpourri from the works of Puccini. Next moment the sugary, sentimental melodies began.

"Strange contrast!" said Ingram. "Here are we sitting warm and cosy, our ears pleasantly tickled with these little baby tunes and outside is the great storm growing more violent every moment, and swirling round the austere cliffs of the Ungeheuerhorn: the Horror-Horn, as indeed it was to me."

"I want to hear all about it," I said. "Every detail: make a short story long, if it's short. I want to know why it's your Horror-Horn?"

"Well, Chanton and I (he was my guide) used to spend days prowling about the cliffs, making a little progress on one side and then being stopped, and gaining perhaps five hundred feet on another side and then being confronted by some insuperable obstacle, till the day when by luck we found the route. Chanton never liked the job, for some reason that I could not fathom.

It was not because of the difficulty or danger of the climbing, for he was the most fearless man I have ever met when dealing with rocks and ice, but he was always insistent that we should get off the mountain and back to the Blumen hut before sunset. He was scarcely easy even when we had got back to shelter and locked and barred the door, and I well remember one night when, as we ate our supper, we heard some animal, a wolf probably, howling somewhere out in the night. A positive panic seized him, and I don't think he closed his eyes till morning. It struck me then that there might be some grisly legend about the mountain, connected possibly with its name, and next day I asked him why the peak was called the Horror-Horn. He put the question off at first, and said that, like the Schreckhorn,[47] its name was due to its precipices and falling stones; but when I pressed him further he acknowledged that there was a legend about it, which his father had told him. There were creatures, so it was supposed, that lived in its caves, things human in shape, and covered, except for the face and hands, with long black hair. They were dwarfs in size, four feet high or thereabouts, but of prodigious strength and agility, remnants of some wild primeval race. It seemed that they were still in an upward stage of evolution, or so I guessed, for the story ran that sometimes girls had been carried off by them, not as prey, and not for any such fate as for those captured by cannibals, but to be bred from. Young men also had been raped by them, to be mated with the females of their tribe. All this looked as if the crea-

---

47. The Fright-Horn in German.

tures, as I said, were tending towards humanity. But naturally I did not believe a word of it, as applied to the conditions of the present day. Centuries ago, conceivably, there may have been such beings, and, with the extraordinary tenacity of tradition, the news of this had been handed down and was still current round the hearths of the peasants. As for their numbers, Chanton told me that three had been once seen together by a man who owing to his swiftness on skis had escaped to tell the tale. This man, he averred, was no other than his grandfather, who had been benighted one winter evening as he passed through the dense woods below the Ungeheuerhorn, and Chanton supposed that they had been driven down to these lower altitudes in search of food during severe winter weather, for otherwise the recorded sights of them had always taken place among the rocks of the peak itself. They had pursued his grandfather, then a young man, at an extraordinarily swift canter, running sometimes upright as men run, sometimes on all-fours in the manner of beasts, and their howls were just such as that we had heard that night in the Blumen hut. Such at any rate was the story Chanton told me, and, like you, I regarded it as the very moonshine of superstition. But the very next day I had reason to reconsider my judgment about it.

"It was on that day that after a week of exploration we hit on the only route at present known to the top of our peak. We started as soon as there was light enough to climb by, for, as you may guess, on very difficult rocks it is impossible to climb by lantern or moonlight. We hit on the long fissure I have spoken of, we explored the ledge which from below seemed to end in nothingness, and with an hour's step-cutting ascended the couloir which led upwards from it. From there onwards it was a rock-climb, certainly of considerable difficulty, but with no heart-breaking discoveries ahead, and it was about nine in the morning that we stood on the top. We did not wait there long, for that side of the mountain is raked by falling stones loosened, when the sun grows hot, from the ice that holds them, and we made haste to pass the ledge where the falls are most frequent. After that there was the long fissure to descend, a matter of no great difficulty, and we were at the end of our work by midday, both of us, as you may imagine, in the state of the highest elation.

"A long and tiresome scramble among the huge boulders at the foot of the cliff then lay before us. Here the hill-side is very porous and great caves extend far into the mountain. We had unroped at the base of the fissure, and were picking our way as seemed good to either of us among these fallen rocks, many of them bigger than an ordinary house, when, on coming round the corner of one of these, I saw that which made it clear that the stories Chanton had told me were no figment of traditional superstition.

"Not twenty yards in front of me lay one of the beings of which he had spoken. There it sprawled naked and basking on its back with face turned up to the sun, which its narrow eyes regarded unwinking. In form it was completely human, but the growth of hair that covered limbs and trunk alike almost completely hid the sun-tanned skin beneath. But its face, save for the down on its cheeks and chin, was hairless, and I looked on a countenance the sensual and malevolent bestiality of which froze me with horror. Had the creature been an animal, one would have felt scarcely a shudder at the gross animalism of it; the horror lay in the fact that it was a man. There lay by it a couple of gnawed bones, and, its meal finished, it was lazily licking its protuberant lips, from which came a purring murmur of content. With one hand it scratched the thick hair on its belly, in the other it held one of these bones, which presently split in half beneath the pressure of its finger and thumb. But my horror was not based on the information of what happened to those men whom these creatures caught, it was due only to my proximity to a thing so human and so infernal. The peak, of which the ascent had a moment ago filled us with such elated satisfaction, became to me an Ungeheuerhorn indeed, for it was the home of beings more awful than the delirium of nightmare could ever have conceived.

"Chanton was a dozen paces behind me, and with a backward wave of my hand I caused him to halt. Then withdrawing myself with infinite precaution, so as not to attract the gaze of that basking creature, I slipped back round the rock, whispered to him what I had seen, and with blanched faces we made a long detour, peering round every corner, and crouching low, not knowing that at any step we might not come upon another of these beings, or that from the mouth of one of these caves in the mountain-side there might not appear another of those hairless and dreadful faces, with perhaps this time the breasts and insignia of womanhood. That would have been the worst of all.

"Luck favoured us, for we made our way among the boulders and shifting stones, the rattle of which might at any moment have betrayed us, without a repetition of my experience, and once among the trees we ran as if the Furies themselves were in pursuit. Well now did I understand, though I dare say I cannot convey, the qualms of Chanton's mind when he spoke to me of these creatures. Their very humanity was what made them so terrible, the fact that they were of the same race as ourselves, but of a type so abysmally degraded that the most brutal and inhuman of men would have seemed angelic in comparison."

The music of the small band was over before he had finished the narrative, and the chattering groups round the tea-table had dispersed. He paused a moment.

"There was a horror of the spirit," he said, "which I experienced then, from which, I verily believe, I have never entirely recovered. I saw then how terrible a living thing could be, and how terrible, in consequence, was life itself. In us all I suppose lurks some inherited germ of that ineffable bestiality, and who knows whether, sterile as it has apparently become in the course of centuries, it might not fructify again. When I saw that creature sun itself, I looked into the abyss out of which we have crawled. And these creatures are trying to crawl out of it now, if they exist any longer. Certainly for the last twenty years there has been no record of their being seen, until we come to this story of the footprint seen by the climbers on Everest. If that is authentic, if the party did not mistake the footprint of some bear, or what not, for a human tread, it seems as if still this bestranded remnant of mankind is in existence."

Now, Ingram had told his story well; but sitting in this warm and civilised room, the horror which he had clearly felt had not communicated itself to me in any very vivid manner. Intellectually, I agreed, I could appreciate his horror, but certainly my spirit felt no shudder of interior comprehension.

"But it is odd," I said, "that your keen interest in physiology did not disperse your qualms. You were looking, so I take it, at some form of man more remote probably than the earliest human remains. Did not something inside you say 'This is of absorbing significance'?"

He shook his head.

"No: I only wanted to get away," said he. "It was not, as I have told you, the terror of what, according to Chanton's story, might await us if we were captured; it was sheer horror at the creature itself. I quaked at it."

The snowstorm and the gale increased in violence that night, and I slept uneasily, plucked again and again from slumber by the fierce battling of the wind that shook my windows as if with an imperious demand for admittance. It came in billowy gusts, with strange noises intermingled with it as for a moment it abated, with flutings and moanings that rose to shrieks as the fury of it returned. These noises, no doubt, mingled themselves with my drowsed and sleepy consciousness, and once I tore myself out of nightmare, imagining that the creatures of the Horror-Horn had gained footing on my balcony and were rattling at the window-bolts. But before morning the gale had died away, and I awoke to see the snow falling dense and fast in a windless air. For three days it continued, without intermission, and with its cessation there came a frost such as I have never felt before. Fifty degrees[48] were registered one night, and more the next, and what the cold must have been on the cliffs of the Ungeheuerhorn I cannot imagine. Sufficient, so I thought, to have made an end altogether of its secret inhabitants: my cousin, on that day twenty years ago, had missed an opportunity for study which would probably never fall again either to him or another.

I received one morning a letter from a friend saying that he had arrived at the neighbouring winter resort of St. Luigi, and proposing that I should come over for a morning's skating and lunch afterwards. The place was not more than a couple of miles off, if one took the path over the low, pine-clad foot-hills above which lay the steep woods below the first rocky slopes of the Ungeheuerhorn; and accordingly, with a knapsack containing skates on my back, I went on skis over the wooded slopes and down by an easy descent again on to St. Luigi. The day was overcast, clouds entirely obscured the higher peaks though the sun was visible, pale and unluminous, through the mists. But as the morning went on, it gained the upper hand, and I slid down into St. Luigi beneath a sparkling firmament.

---

48. "Fifty degrees of frost" means fifty degrees below freezing.

We skated and lunched, and then, since it looked as if thick weather was coming up again, I set out early about three o'clock for my return journey.

Hardly had I got into the woods when the clouds gathered thick above, and streamers and skeins of them began to descend among the pines through which my path threaded its way. In ten minutes more their opacity had so increased that I could hardly see a couple of yards in front of me. Very soon I became aware that I must have got off the path, for snow-cowled shrubs lay directly in my way, and, casting back to find it again, I got altogether confused as to direction. But, though progress was difficult, I knew I had only to keep on the ascent, and presently I should come to the brow of these low foot-hills, and descend into the open valley where Alhubel stood. So on I went, stumbling and sliding over obstacles, and unable, owing to the thickness of the snow, to take off my skis, for I should have sunk over the knees at each step. Still the ascent continued, and looking at my watch I saw that I had already been near an hour on my way from St. Luigi, a period more than sufficient to complete my whole journey. But still I stuck to my idea that though I had certainly strayed far from my proper route a few minutes more must surely see me over the top of the upward way, and I should find the ground declining into the next valley. About now, too, I noticed that the mists were growing suffused with rose-colour, and, though the inference was that it must be close on sunset, there was consolation in the fact that they were there and might lift at any moment and disclose to me my whereabouts. But the fact that night would soon be on me made it needful to bar my mind against that despair of loneliness which so eats out the heart of a man who is lost in woods or on mountain-side, that, though still there is plenty of vigour in his limbs, his nervous force is sapped, and he can do no more than lie down and abandon himself to whatever fate may await him... And then I heard that which made the thought of loneliness seem bliss indeed, for there was a worse fate than loneliness. What I heard resembled the howl of a wolf, and it came from not far in front of me where the ridge—was it a ridge?—still rose higher in vestment of pines.

From behind me came a sudden puff of wind, which shook the frozen snow from the drooping pine-branches, and swept away the mists as a broom sweeps the dust from the floor. Radiant above me were the unclouded skies, already charged with the red of the sunset, and in front I saw that I had come to the very edge of the wood through which I had wandered so long. But it was no valley into which I had penetrated, for there right ahead of me rose the steep slope of boulders and rocks soaring upwards to the foot of the Ungeheuerhorn. What, then, was that cry of a wolf which had made my heart stand still? I saw.

Not twenty yards from me was a fallen tree, and leaning against the trunk of it was one of the denizens of the Horror-Horn, and it was a woman. She was enveloped in a thick growth of hair grey and tufted, and from her head it streamed down over her shoulders and her bosom, from which hung withered and pendulous breasts. And looking on her face I comprehended not with my mind alone, but with a shudder of my spirit, what Ingram had felt. Never had nightmare fashioned so terrible a countenance; the beauty of sun and stars and of the beasts of the field and the kindly race of men could not atone for so hellish an incarnation of the spirit of life. A fathomless bestiality modelled the slavering mouth and the narrow eyes; I looked into the abyss itself and knew that out of that abyss on the edge of which I leaned the generations of men had climbed. What if that ledge crumbled in front of me and pitched me headlong into its nethermost depths?...

In one hand she held by the horns a chamois that kicked and struggled. A blow from its hindleg caught her withered thigh, and with a grunt of anger she seized the leg in her other hand, and, as a man may pull from its sheath a stem of meadow-grass, she plucked it off the body, leaving the torn skin hanging round the gaping wound. Then putting the red, bleeding member to her mouth she sucked at it as a child sucks a stick of sweetmeat. Through flesh and gristle her short, brown teeth penetrated, and she licked her lips with a sound of purring. Then dropping the leg by her side, she looked again at the body of the prey now quivering in its death-convulsion, and with finger and thumb gouged out one of its eyes. She snapped her teeth on it, and it cracked like a soft-shelled nut.

It must have been but a few seconds that I stood watching her, in some indescribable catalepsy of terror, while through my brain there pealed the panic-command of my mind to my stricken limbs "Begone, begone, while there is time." Then, recovering the power of my joints and muscles, I tried to slip behind a tree and hide myself from this apparition. But the woman— shall I say?—must have caught my stir of movement, for she raised her eyes from her living feast and saw me. She craned forward her neck, she dropped her prey, and half rising began to move towards me. As she did this, she opened her mouth, and gave forth a howl such as I had heard a moment before. It was answered by another, but faintly and distantly.

Sliding and slipping, with the toes of my skis tripping in the obstacles below the snow, I plunged forward down the hill between the pine-trunks. The low sun already sinking behind some rampart of mountain in the west reddened the snow and the pines with its ultimate rays. My knapsack with the skates in it swung to and fro on my back, one ski-stick had already been twitched out of my hand by a fallen branch of pine, but not a second's pause could I allow myself to recover it. I gave no glance behind, and I knew not at what pace my pursuer was on my track, or indeed whether any pursued at all, for my whole mind and energy, now working at full power again under the stress of my panic, was devoted to getting away down the hill and out of the wood as swiftly as my limbs could bear me. For a little while I heard nothing but the hissing snow of my headlong passage, and the rustle of the covered undergrowth beneath my feet, and then, from close at hand behind me, once more the wolf-howl sounded and I heard the plunging of footsteps other than my own.

The strap of my knapsack had shifted, and as my skates swung to and fro on my back it chafed and pressed on my throat, hindering free passage of air, of which, God knew, my labouring lungs were in dire need, and without pausing I slipped it free from my neck, and held it in the hand from which my ski-stick had been jerked. I seemed to go a little more easily for this adjustment, and now, not so far distant, I could see below me the path from which I had strayed. If only I could reach that, the smoother going would surely enable me to out-distance my pursuer, who even on the rougher ground was but slowly overhauling me, and at the sight of that riband stretching unimpeded downhill, a ray of hope pierced the black panic of my soul. With that came the desire, keen and insistent, to see who or what it was that was on my tracks, and I spared a backward glance. It was she, the hag whom I had seen at her gruesome meal; her long grey hair flew out behind her, her mouth chattered and gibbered, her fingers made grabbing movements, as if already they closed on me.

But the path was now at hand, and the nearness of it I suppose made me incautious. A hump of snow-covered bush lay in my path, and, thinking I could jump over it, I tripped and fell, smothering myself in snow. I heard a maniac noise, half scream, half laugh, from close behind, and before I could recover myself the grabbing fingers were at my neck, as if a steel vice had closed there. But my right hand in which I held my knapsack of skates was free, and with a blind back-handed movement I whirled it behind me at the full length of its strap, and knew that my desperate blow had found its billet somewhere. Even before I could look round I felt the grip on my neck relax, and something subsided into the very bush which had entangled me. I recovered my feet and turned.

There she lay, twitching and quivering. The heel of one of my skates piercing the thin alpaca of the knapsack had hit her full on the temple, from which the blood was pouring, but a hundred yards away I could see another such figure coming downwards on my tracks, leaping and bounding. At that panic rose again within me, and I sped off down the white smooth path that led to the lights of the village already beckoning. Never once did I pause in my headlong going: there was no safety until I was back among the haunts of men. I flung myself against the door of the hotel, and screamed for admittance, though I had but to turn the handle and enter; and once more as when Ingram had told his tale, there was the sound of the band, and the chatter of voices, and there, too, was he himself, who looked up and then rose swiftly to his feet as I made my clattering entrance.

"I have seen them too," I cried. "Look at my knapsack. Is there not blood on it? It is the blood of one of them, a woman, a hag, who tore off the leg of a chamois as I looked, and pursued me through the accursed wood. I—"

Whether it was I who spun round, or the room which seemed to spin round me, I knew not, but I heard myself falling, collapsed on the floor, and the next time that I was conscious at all I was in bed. There was

Ingram there, who told me that I was quite safe, and another man, a stranger, who pricked my arm with the nozzle of a syringe, and reassured me...

A day or two later I gave a coherent account of my adventure, and three or four men, armed with guns, went over my traces. They found the bush in which I had stumbled, with a pool of blood which had soaked into the snow, and, still following my ski-tracks, they came on the body of a chamois, from which had been torn one of its hindlegs and one eye-socket was empty. That is all the corroboration of my story that I can give the reader, and for myself I imagine that the creature which pursued me was either not killed by my blow or that her fellows removed her body... Anyhow, it is open to the incredulous to prowl about the caves of the Ungeheuerhorn, and see if anything occurs that may convince them.

Bibliography

Benson, E. F. "A Comedy of Styles." *The Windsor Magazine* 39, no. 230 (February 1914): 331–335.

———. *English Figure Skating: A Guide to the Theory and Practice of Skating in the English Style.* London: G. Bell and Sons, 1908.

———. *Mr. Teddy.* London: T. Fisher Unwin, Ltd., 1917.

———. *Our Family Affairs, 1867–1896.* New York: George H. Doran, c. 1921.

———. *Sketches from Marlborough.* Marlborough: Chas. Perkins, 1888.

———. *The Babe, B.A.: Being the Uneventful History of a Young Gentleman at Cambridge University.* New York: G. P. Putnam's Sons, 1896.

———. *The Book of Months.* London: William Heinemann, 1903.

———. "The Peerage Cure." *The Windsor Magazine* 64, no. 379 (July 1926): 119–124.

———. *The Room in the Tower and Other Stories.* 2nd edition. London: Mills and Boon, 1912.

———. *The Tortoise.* New York: George H. Doran Company, 1917.

Benson, E. F. *Visible and Invisible.* London: Hutchinson and Co., 1923.

———. "Winter Pastimes." *The Windsor Magazine* 33, no. 192 (1911): 157–166.

———. *Winter Sports in Switzerland.* London: George Allen and Company, 1913.

Crawley, A. E. "English Figure-Skating." *The Saturday Review of Politics, Literature, Science and Art* 116 (February 1913): 235–236.

Goldhill, Simon. *A Very Queer Family Indeed: Sex, Religion, and the Bensons in Victorian Britain.* Chicago: University of Chicago Press, 2016.

Hines, James R. *The English Style: Figure Skating's Oldest Tradition.* Westwood, MA: Neponset River Press, 2008.

Lowther, Henry C. *English Skating: Edges and Striking, Principle of Skating Turns, Combined Figure Skating.* Edited by B. A. Thurber. Evanston, IL: Skating History Press, 2019.

Masters, Brian. *The Life of E. F. Benson.* London: Chatto and Windus, 1991.

"Grindelwald Skating Club." *The Field* 99, no. 2567 (March 1902): 328.

"Grindelwald Skating Club." *The Field* 103, no. 2667 (February 1904): 203.

"National Skating Association—Figure Skating Department." *The Field* 82, no. 2132 (November 1893): 697.

"Skating and Tobagganing at Davos." *The Field* 103, no. 2664 (January 1904): 106.

"Skating at St. Moritz: The Holland Challenge Bowl." *The Field* 101, no. 2617 (February 1903): 307.

"Skating in Switzerland." *The Field* 118, no. 2924 (January 1909): 64.

Illustration credits

Digitized by the University of Michigan and provided courtesy of HathiTrust unless otherwise noted.

1–2: Photos from *Our Family Affairs, 1867–1896.* Courtesy of Wikimedia Commons.

3: Photo by B. A. Thurber of the Dowler skates in her collection. Courtesy of B. A. Thurber.

4–6: Drawings by Wilmot Lunt from "The Peerage Cure," 119, 122–132. Courtesy of the Internet Archive.

7: Photo by "Topical" from "Winter Pastimes," 157.

8: Photo by Ballance, St. Moritz, from "Winter Pastimes," 158.

9–10: Photos by "Topical" from "Winter Pastimes," 159.

11–18: Photos by Ballance, St. Moritz, from "Winter Pastimes," 160–163.

19: Photo by "Topical" from "Winter Pastimes," 164.

20: Photo by Ballance, St. Moritz, from "Winter Pastimes," 164.

21–22: Photos by "Topical" from "Winter Pastimes," 165–166.

23–24: Drawings by Charles Peares from "A Comedy of Styles," 331, 333. Digitized by Google Books.

www.ingramcontent.com/pod-product-compliance
Lightning Source LLC
Chambersburg PA
CBHW050535190726

48284CB00003B/1086